MW00437605

Five Stars for Liz Crowe's Stewart Realty Series

"Gut-wrenching and heartbreaking, Sweat Equity is a roller coaster ride of emotions, taking you through a colossal train wreck of a relationship…then has you begging to go again… Ms. Crowe has done an outstanding job of making you feel every verbal slap, every erotic touch, and every heartbreaking and colossal screw up from beginning to end. The sex in the book is incredible…it's fast, furious, angry, elemental and animalistic. There are a lot of erotic encounters in Sweat Equity, including some super fabulous M/M scenes with Sara's brother Blake and his partner Rob, but none are over the top or placed in as filler for the "real" plot. For its realistic story line and dialogue, ability to make me connect with every single character in the book and the capacity to both piss me off and turn me on simultaneously, Sweat Equity is much deserving of a *JERR Gold Star Award*. I am waiting anxiously for Ms. Crowe's third installment in the *Stewart Realty* series with bated, and outraged, breath."

~ *Just Erotic Romance Reviews*

"Hands down, one of my favorite reads of 2012 and has earned a much deserved 5 stars! I cannot find the words to accurately convey how much I loved this book. This series is so realistic, raw, emotional, mouth-watering hot – but I absolutely love it."

~*Hesperia Loves Books*

"Crowe has a talent for bringing to the page characters with confused, conflicting emotions who don't even realize they are creating their own misery by trying so hard to avoid broken hearts – just like real life! Jack and Sara make misstep after misstep until I wanted to scream at them to get it together already. They love each other so much and yet make their lives so hard."

~ *My Book Addiction Reviews*

"Sara and Jack burn up the pages of Sweat Equity, together and apart, as they fight to get each other out of their hearts. The sex scenes sizzle and will make you breathless. But, it is the push and pull of attraction between Sara and Jack that will drive you up the wall. I became very frustrated with Jack's inability to put his feelings into words. I wanted him to get back with Sara but he kept saying and doing the wrong thing. I can't wait until the Closing Costs come out to see what happens with them and their romance."

~ Sizzling Hot Reviews

"The characters were appealing and well-developed; the writing impressed me from the first page. I think Jack and Sara have the potential to be a super couple with explosive chemistry and sex that is off the charts hot. However, I did want more of the BDSM in their relationship. It was obvious Sara wanted it too, but Jack was never fully able to let go and be his true self. Liz Crowe was a new author to me and I would definitely read other books by her. Her style flows which makes for a great, easy read with really hot sex."

~ Guilty Pleasures Reviews

"It's highly emotional with likable characters doing unlikable things, but I was never bored and was totally drawn into this world waiting with bated breath for the next part of this rollercoaster ride to romance. Daily soap operas on TV pale in comparison to what Liz Crowe has created here! With so many romances left in limbo and a jaw dropping incident coming at the very end of this book (which I knew was coming but didn't diminish the shock), I'm on pins and needles waiting to read the concluding book in this pull-out-your-hair-tug-out-your-heart series."

~ Words of Wisdom from the Scarf Princess

Other Liz Crowe Books
From Sizzlin' Books:

Stewart Realty Series:
Floor Time
Sweat Equity
Closing Costs
Essence of Time

Standalone Titles:
Vegas Miracle

Coming Soon:
Escalation Clause (Stewart Realty Book 5)

You can find out more about Liz Crowe and her
books (including a complete backlist)
on her website: www.lizcrowe.com

 Sizzlin' Books is a Division of Tri Destiny Publishing

Find us online at www.sizzlinbooks.com

Liz Crowe

SWEAT *Equity*

Sizzlin' Books
A Division of Tri Destiny Publishing

If you have purchased this book without its cover, be aware that it is most probably stolen and that neither the author nor the publishers were paid for their work.

This book is a work of fiction. All characters, names, storylines, and businesses are the work product of the author or fictitiously used and therefore any resemblance to any actual people, alive or dead, places, and businesses is entirely coincidental.

Sweat Equity (Stewart Realty Book 2)

A *Sizzlin' Book* published by permission of the author

Printing History
Sizzlin' Books Edition February, 2012

Copyright © 2012 by Liz Crowe
Cover Art and Design by JJ Silver Designs

All rights reserved.
This book, or parts thereof, may not be reproduced
in any form without permission.

For information address: *Sizzlin' Books*
a division of Tri Destiny Publishing
P.O. Box 330 Arcola, IL 61910

Visit our website at
www.sizzlinbooks.com

ISBN: 978-0-9569669-9-5
Sizzlin'Books are published by Tri Destiny Publishing

Printed in the United States of America

For Susan

Thanks for your amazing support

and unquestioning loyalty

PROLOGUE

New Year's Day

Sara sat, blanket clutched to her breasts, breathing heavy with sweat trickling down her neck. She was shocked the entire resort didn't awake from her scream. Glancing over at the sleeping man next to her, she tried to let his presence soothe as it normally did. He snored and rolled over onto his side, flinging an arm across her lap.

The tall woman from her dream would not fade. "You can't trust him Sara. Believe me. He only gave you that ring because he couldn't have you any other way. He'll be up to his old tricks soon; mark my words." The vision of the dream woman turning to a tall, familiar dark-haired man and wrapping her lean body against his, made Sara clench her eyes shut. Dreams were supposed to fade once you woke, but this one had her in its clutches and would not let go.

She crawled out from under Jack's arm and the tangle of sheets and sat on the edge of the bed, letting the ocean air rustling through the sheer window coverings cool her overheated skin. The moonlight caught the diamond she wore, making her wince when it hit her square in the eye with its brilliance. Swallowing hard, she padded over to the enormous bathroom, shut the door and slid to the floor, letting tears roll down her face. Evidence of the intense session they'd shared last night lay all around her: Soft leather restraints, a bottle of expensive champagne, a vibrator and a bottle of lubricant. She squirmed on the floor, sore in places she didn't know she had.

Jack certainly knew how to throw a party. She brushed the tears away berating herself.

You liked it. Don't be such a hypocrite. You love giving him control over you this way.

The fact that he'd whisked her away on a surprise New Year's Eve junket to St. Bart's, to this remote, secluded and ultra-exclusive resort that "supported" their lifestyle choice had shocked the shit out of her at first. But by the time he'd worked her into a frenzy on the private jet and they'd emerged in the paradise of seventy-degree weather, ocean breezes and more of his fingers, lips, tongue and cock, she gave into it, loving every breathless minute.

"Hey," a soft knock and the sound of his deep, morning gravelly voice made her startle. "What's up in there?"

She stood, splashed water on her face and opened the door, smile fixed on her face. He frowned and pulled her into his arms. She sighed, letting the mysterious way he calmed her by his sheer presence work its magic. It was so strange, amazingly erotic, highly charged, and seemingly perfect – but for the dreams.

"I have an idea," he spoke into her hair.

"Huh, if it involves my ass again, we'd better wait twenty four hours." She giggled at his groan, felt his cock stir against her and suppressed her own surge of horniness.

"Seriously, I may not sit for a week. Not that I'm complaining."

"I am serious." He stepped back, took her face between his hands. His deep blue gaze did its usual song and dance on her emotions. "Marry me."

"I already said yes to that remember?" She flashed the giant ring she still couldn't adjust to on her finger. "Under duress I might add."

He smiled, ran a finger over her lips. "No. Today. Here."

She frowned at him, her brain skipping ahead to what exactly that meant. No big wedding. No parental or brotherly stress. Tying herself to this man, forever, without friends or family to witness. Tempting.

"I can't." She shrugged his hands off her and walked over to the window, winding a soft robe around her nudity.

"Why not?" His hands on her shoulders encouraged her to lean against his tall, firm body. "Why go through the torture of planning an event we know will be stressful as hell for everybody involved? Besides, I'm gonna be so busy with this new building thing, I won't really be much help. And I just think…" he leaned down to brush a kiss against her cheek, making her shiver. "I'm afraid we aren't cut out for the whole big wedding thing. You know?"

"No, we'll be fine. I'll plan. You nod your head at the appropriate moments. I don't need you to do much more than that, other than show up at the right hour in the right suit."

He snorted and flopped down in a large leather chair. "Yeah, that and write checks."

She rolled her eyes. "No, I told you my dad would pay…"

"Stop. Right there. We discussed this already. See; look at us, fighting already. C'mere you sexy beast," he yanked her down onto his lap, covered her protests with his lips, letting his hands roam under the robe, pulling it off her shoulders.

"Jack," she whispered, threading her hands in his thick hair, letting him take her again, away from a potential conflict with his body. "You may be right, but, I can't do that to my mom. She wants me to have this moment, the walk-down-the-aisle moment, and I think I do too, okay?"

"Baby, I want whatever you want, as long as it makes you happy." She pushed his face up off its current mission towards her breasts, making him look at her.

"Do you really mean that?"

He sighed, and wrapped his arms tight around her, holding her so close she heard his beating heart. "I do. There. See? I even know the right words."

"But…" She rose from his lap, unwilling to let this go yet. "I'm still worried, I mean, you sprung this on me and I need to know."

He stood in front of her, took both her hands. "You can trust me. I promise even if you are denying me the simple joy of a quickie wedding in paradise." His grin was contagious. She shoved the misgivings that cropped up and haunted her for hours every time she had that same dream into a small corner of her mind and wrapped her arms around his neck, sucked in a deep breath of his now familiar scent, and kissed him, long and deep.

He gripped her ass, pulled her legs up around his body and dove in, no preamble, as he dropped her onto the bed. She gasped. "Wait! No condom." He sighed and eased in further, silencing her with his lips. *Oh well, it wasn't a dangerous week for that and damn did it feel good.* She cried out his name repeatedly, logic lost once in the swirl of physical satisfaction that only Jack could provide.

CHAPTER ONE

Four Months Later

Jack woke with a start, and immediately regretted it. The hangover that had been lying in wait pounced hard, landing somewhere between his eyes. Groaning, he rolled over and found himself on the floor, trying not to puke all over his expensive Turkish rug. He sat back against the couch and tried to get his bearings. When the room cooperated by holding still, he ran a shaking hand over his eyes and stood. Leaving explanations for why in the hell he woke up on the couch, still half-dressed in pants and an unbuttoned blue shirt, for a time when he gave a shit, he stumbled into the kitchen. The sun streaming through the large window smacked him upside the head, bringing fresh life to the agony.

"Fuck." He sucked back about a gallon of water and leaned against the cold granite counter top. "No, seriously. Fuck." He yanked his phone out of his pocket and squinted at the missed calls from nearly an hour before. It was Saturday but, for a change, he didn't have any serious work to do until nearly four. A few fumbling minutes later the comforting sounds and aroma of a coffee-fix floated around him. He looked up when the shower noises from the master bathroom stopped.

Oh hell.

Sara.

It came rushing back in bursts of idiocy and epic drunkenness. They'd both been that way after a friend's party, but once home she'd started in on the wedding plans again, and he'd lost it. He stared at his blood-red eyes in the downstairs bathroom mirror. In the way of most disagreements fueled by stress and alcohol, he barely remembered how it started. But he had full knowledge of how it ended. He groaned. He had been a colossal prick. That much he remembered with crystal clarity. He'd been tired, not wanting to go out after a week of unbelievable frustration at City Hall.

Maybe he wasn't cut out for this total commitment thing. He'd been zoning out every time she brought up any detail of the "classy" event she wanted to pull off in about six months. "Classy" seemed to mean "horrifically expensive" if his newly minted Wedding Decoder Ring worked right. Not that they weren't more than capable of paying for all the "delicate white lilies" on all the country club tables and top of the line videographer themselves, but last night she'd informed Jack that her father, the estimable Doctor Matthew Clay Thornton, wanted to pay for his only daughter's nuptial ceremony. He had flown in from Florida with Sara's mother for a nice, intimate dinner with Sara and her fiancé.

After the week he'd spent in the city planning offices trying to convince a bunch of pinheaded politicians that the massive renovation of a long-abandoned office building on a busy downtown corner would actually be good for their city, he had not a single ounce of patience left. Those assholes had hemmed and hawed him into nearly fifty grand more in architect's fees. Yet, he still had no approval. And he'd agreed to walk down the proverbial aisle a mere week after the scheduled building opening and gala party he wanted to throw – an opening that now looked jeopardized if not decimated by pin-headed bureaucrats.

"Ah, hell." He pushed himself away from the sink, the need to hurl the three bottles of red wine and two ill-considered bourbons from last night out of his system. He had to face this. He'd said some colossally stupid things. He'd been avoiding the wedding talk like a trooper, saying stupid shit like, "Just tell me when and where and I'll be there in the dark suit," long enough. He'd sprung the proposal on her. It had been, no, it *was*, what he wanted: Sara, in his life, forever and ever, until death, or whatever.

If only she'd just agreed to marry him at the resort, the arguments would be a nonissue. They'd had such a great time learning their way around the milder elements of the BDSM fun while they were there. It had been perfect. Eloping would have kept all this stress out of his life.

But she was being so bloody stubborn on this thing. He knew it has to be tough for her, submitting to him on any level, and he admired her for it. But he felt his control slipping and that pissed him off too. He couldn't, or wouldn't, exert the full force of his naturally dominating nature on her. She wasn't ready for that. Maybe he wasn't either.

Jack squinted at himself once more. Lines covered his face from lying pressed against the couch arm all night. Jaw covered in rough stubble, thick hair, still black as night, having been blessed by some gene which avoided the salt-and-pepper look. He ran a hand over his dry lips and squared his shoulders. Apologies for bullshit behavior usually came pretty easy. Still, something kept him downstairs, unable to form the right words. He made his way back to the kitchen, poured some coffee into a heavy stoneware mug and sighed.

Sara toweled off, her mind focusing on the long list of houses she had to show a new client in a couple of hours, her heart still clenched in anger. She'd passed out, alone, in Jack's huge bed. The sunlight caught the diamond on her left hand, throwing prisms of light around the large bathroom. She'd never put much stock in jewelry, or flowers, or any of the usual shit women seemed to get off on. So, when Jack Gordon, the man she'd been literally fucking around with for months, had sprung a marriage proposal on her in front of their entire company last fall she'd been shocked, to say the least. She stared at the four-carat rock on her finger. It was a work of art-deco beauty. The best that money could buy.

Typical Jack.

Jack's handsome face, strong body, snapping blue eyes, incredible sales skills–and masterful talent with his lips, hands, tongue, everything about him had compelled her for months; driving her, making her work harder, turning into a newer, better version of herself. But every day brought more doubt about her decision to marry him. She wrapped her body in the large white towel and brushed her teeth, listening for sounds of life downstairs. He had even made her more organized, tidier. Something about him made her want to push herself harder, be better. It made her completely insane with a combination of frustration and something resembling jealousy.

Damn they'd said some ugly stuff to each other. She shuddered, remembering calling him "no better than a man-shaped dildo" at one point. Accusing him of things just short of the Kennedy assassination and global warming. He'd been such a gigantic prick about meeting her parents and spent the evening sulky and uncommunicative with their friends. She'd simply exploded when they got home. He had met her halfway no doubt about it.

What was his problem? He'd made it clear this "wedding crap" was hers to manage. He'd said he needed to pay for it and would write checks for whatever she wanted. But when it came time to start doing so he'd balked, questioning everything she'd arranged, making her doubt herself. The doubt about her ability to plan a simple wedding had leached over into a lot of worry about the whole situation. She sighed, listening again for noise from downstairs.

When her mother called last week and informed her that they wanted to spend the weekend in Ann Arbor so her father could give her the money for the wedding, she'd been relieved. No more answering to Jack. Something in her knew that wasn't right. They were supposed to be husband and wife and learning to communicate about shit like this. Sara took another sip from her water bottle, wincing at the queasy feeling in her gut from previous night's combination of over indulgence and anger. It felt impossible now. The magic date they'd set: November eighth. One week after the new downtown project opened. The project she'd gotten as deeply into as he had, with many late nights spent poring over drawings, contemplating possibilities of retail versus residential versus rentals.

Maybe her brother was right. Blake had given a whole new meaning to "hate," specifically as it related to Jack Gordon. Claimed Jack would be nothing but a serial cheater; couldn't resist women and would never settle for just one. After she'd agreed to marry him, Blake had backed off from the vitriol, but had once suggested that two people as alike as she and Jack would have nothing but misery ahead of them. That comment stuck with her for weeks. The very concept seemed ludicrous, even insulting. She was not like Jack. No way. But the more they clashed, the more she wondered.

Tears threatened at the thought of calling it off, but the last week or so she'd been questioning her sanity. The office gossip about Jack had ramped up and even taken on a bitter tone as all the women, who'd hoped to be in her four-carat-wearing shoes, started griping, most of it reaching her ears. The man obviously had not been able to keep that impressive cock in his pants much; that had become crystal clear.

He'd taught her so much about how relinquishing her tight control to him was a pure turn on, fueling her libido in ways she had no idea were possible. It also terrified her at the same time. Ceding control like that, to a man like Jack, inevitably left her feeling cold, scared and vulnerable. He'd made a promise to her. She would never, ever be left unsatisfied or made to feel humiliated by anything they did. He'd kept his promise. However, at times, she felt herself shut down afterward, as if that sort of trust was something she had no idea how to give, or get.

The niggling words "you two are too much alike to work" kept coming back, tickling her brain, making her antsy.

Damn Blake

After rubbing her hair with styling gel, she blinked the tears back and tried to focus on the day ahead. Saturdays were notoriously long days for realtors, and today promised to be a doozy. To top it off, she had the pleasure of dinner with her parents, Blake and his partner Rob, and her fiancé to look forward to. That was, if Jack decided to attend. After last night's blow out, she wasn't so sure.

Fuck him.

She grabbed the hair dryer and ignored the growing ache in her chest–the spot she'd come to call Jack's place. He alone had the ability to fill it with joy and ecstasy one moment, fury and frustration the next. He remained a cipher to her. She still knew very little about his family, about which he seemed disinclined to share. He preferred keeping them both "in the here-and-now," which usually meant in bed, on the floor, or back in his office, with his talented body teasing orgasms out of her at his will.

How in the hell could a relationship like that possibly work?

Fortified by caffeine, Jack made his quiet way upstairs. The hair dryer fired up as he entered the bedroom suite. His head still pounded but he knew part of it was from dread. Failure threatened large on his horizon. He knew it and didn't want to subject her to the messiness. The "down the aisle" thing made him numb with terror. The thought of Sara not in his world made him want to lose his lunch. He leaned on the doorjamb, watching her. She'd given him her trust. He'd wanted it–demanded it even. But did he deserve it? Sometimes he wondered.

Christ, what a mess.

Only he had the power to fix it. That kind of responsibility for another person's emotional well-being had been easy for him once, and something he thought he knew how to handle. Lately, with the woman he loved, he had serious doubts.

Her light brown hair formed a curtain over her face as she worked the hair dryer under its many layers. Jack's hands clenched into fists, resisting the urge to bury them in it, drag her to the bed; apologize with his body and not his words.

She'd called him on that too, hadn't she? Yes. She had.

He groaned and looked up at the ceiling, sitting on the edge of the large bed, which was only messed on the side she'd slept in alone.

His "natural prick" had emerged when she'd given him the "dinner-with-the-parents" news after the insufferable party they'd attended at her insistence. He had no desire to meet them, but knew it had to be done. He'd sloshed bourbon into a crystal glass and knocked it back before turning to her and accusing her of ambushing him with that little tidbit. He'd reminded her that he was perfectly capable of paying for their wedding, even if she wanted to ship all two-hundred invitees to fucking St. Bart's on private planes. She had no business involving her father.

She did, didn't she?

The guy had every right to be involved in his only daughter's wedding plans. Even though Jack knew damn good and well,thanks to a conversation with Rob over a few beers, Sara's father was a class-A prick who had been a shitty role model relationship-wise. *Jesus.* He ran a hand over his face again.

Things had quickly devolved from there. She'd had her own shot of brown liquor and accused him of being a man-whore, expressed her unhappiness with the constant stream of gossip about all his escapades from their real estate colleagues. Jack didn't regret much in life, but at that moment, he had nothing but remorse for the women he'd pissed off if their animosity had caused the kind of pain he'd seen in Sara's eyes.

Of course, he couldn't have just said that, could he? Oh no. He'd laughed, like an asshole. Told her to get over it. He was what he was and she damn good and well had partaken of the "Jack fun" herself, hadn't she?

He looked up in time to see her bend over to give her hair a final heat treatment. The sight of her ass up in the air, barely covered by one of his thick towels brought his cock to strict attention. He sucked in a breath, staying out of her line of sight. When she finished with the dryer, and ran a brush through her hair he narrowed his eyes.

Tears.

Great.

She dropped the towel, making Jack's body tingle in anticipation. Lotion next, smoothed over her long, strong legs, across her luscious ass, around her firm breasts. His breath got short, ragged in his ears.

He had to talk, communicate better. His head kept buzzing as he stood, walked into the cavernous bathroom, stood behind her, and put his hands on her smooth shoulders. She looked up into his eyes, gaze flat and noncommittal.

Jack ran both hands down her arms, letting the essence of her infuse his senses. He wanted this, more than he wanted to draw a breath. He wanted her, there, every morning. The concept of screwing it up with his usual bullshit made him nearly blind with fury at himself. But, right then, he wanted nothing more than to touch, to caress, to soothe and kiss.

She didn't respond, just stood stock still as he kept touching, down to her hips and thighs. He moved to her side and put a hand to her cheek, making her turn to face him. Unshed tears glinted in her deep green eyes. He swallowed but words wouldn't form. His lips found hers, his tongue tasted her, and she moaned and molded herself against him, wrapped her arms around his neck as he picked her up and carried her to the bed.

"Jack," she muttered as he pushed her back against the pillows and made his way down her body with his lips.

"Shh," he dipped his tongue into her navel, went lower, and nuzzled the small bit of hair covering her sex. His cock twitched, leaked, ached for the now-familiar connection with her. His brain engaged long enough to acknowledge he'd meet her damn father, suck up properly, and let the guy pay for some of the ceremony. He couldn't lose this woman. He smiled against her pussy as he sucked the hard nub of her clit into his mouth, before plunging two fingers inside her, brushing that magic spot, sending her over the edge. Her juices coated his face and fingers and he licked his way back up, giving each nipple a suck, rubbing the thick head of his cock against her now creamy center.

"Look at me," she whispered. He did, caught off guard by the depth of emotion he found in her gaze. "I love you Jack. I truly do. But, I'm afraid. I'm…oh. God."

Jack let his body speak for him, pressing in, filling her, groaning at the amazing tight glove of her body which enveloped him, milked him, as he eased in and out. She put her hands to his face. As always, the deeper connection he felt with her roared over him, deafening him with urgency and no small amount of fear at letting go. He dove into her body, pressing against her clit, using his hips with small thrusts to drive even deeper. They hadn't used condoms since the New Year's trip and the whole barebacked thing was, in a word, glorious, although they played with fire, and he knew it.

"Tell me." Her voice was low, rasping, and sexy. "Tell me Jack."

"Ah God, Sara," he ground out, as her orgasm gripped his cock, tightening and pulling him over the edge. "I, I love you, oh Christ. Yes!" He pounded hard, felt his world burst into a thousand pieces behind his eyes as his cock jerked and filled her. She cried out with him, and held on, arms and legs wrapped around his body, bringing him utter and complete happiness.

Sara smiled at the man next to her. He'd taken her world and yanked it into his orbit so hard and fast her head still spun some days. God help her she did love him. She put a hand on his sweat-slicked chest, and draped a leg over his. The smell of sex permeated the bedroom. She propped up on her elbow and touched his check.

"Hmm?" his sleepy voice reminded her how much they both needed more shut eye having passed out rather than actually rested last night. He pulled her close. "I'm sorry," he muttered into her hair. "It's just." She nodded into his shoulder. "Shit week, you know. All this wedding talk is not my thing or something. I don't know. I do know I don't deserve you."

"Yeah, that is true. Look, we still have dinner with my parents tonight. My dad is a know-it-all doctor. I dread having the two of you in the same room, frankly, but we have to do it. They're my family and they want to meet you."

She felt him tense beneath her.

"That's fine. I'll be on my best behavior. But I don't want him paying for any of this," he swept a hand towards the small table where she'd piled up magazines and spreadsheets of wedding planning paraphernalia. "I'm doing it. You're grown, not some little girl needing daddy's money anymore."

She bit her lip. "If he wants to I'm not going to stop him. It's his prerogative. Can't you just go with it?" She sat up, swung her legs to the floor.

Dear God he was so unbelievably stubborn!

He sang the same song, different verse, every time. They'd fight, he'd make up by making love to her. She'd let him. They wouldn't talk about it. Again.

Sighing she stood, stretched her sated and tingling body, her mind back on the massive list of shit to do today. Glancing over her shoulder, she allowed herself a long look at the man who would be her husband. His six-foot five-inch frame firm, legs and arms covered with a light dusting of black hair; torso mostly bare, but for a line of jet-black hair beneath his navel leading down to the part of his body that he had, apparently, shared with so many. Her eyes trailed up, to his firm, square jaw, in need of a shave. Her palm itched to reach out, feel the sandpapery rasp of it, keeping him real.

Mine.

How completely unreal this still seemed, even now after he'd given her yet another mind-boggling set of back-to-back orgasms. That should've been solid evidence he was there, with her, "hers" even. But he wasn't. That small voice in her head, the "Old Sara," with its nagging and worry, poked her psyche once again. *You're too alike. It will never work.* Jack's eyes opened, at the sound of his own light snore. His sleepy grin made her smile in spite of her heavy heart.

She was no sap. Her own parent's relationship had made her a cynic to the extreme when it came to men. She knew it. She fully acknowledged her own emotional constipation. Yet, she let the man who currently held her heart in his large, talented hands tug her down onto the bed, into the circle of his arms. His skin, smell, and feel eased her as always. She closed her eyes, just for a few minutes.

CHAPTER TWO

"Why in the hell did you leave it here?" Sara bounded up the steps to Jack's bedroom, having yet to acknowledge as "hers." She yanked his suitcase out of the closet where he'd placed it after his Vegas trip to the National Association of Realtors convention. She still smarted from that week but set her jaw, determined not to bitch or whine about it another minute. The extreme tidiness of Jack's space...*no, her space now*...made the small voice of self-doubt speak a little louder, yet again. She tossed the small black suitcase up on the bed and unzipped it.

"Do you see it? I must have tucked it in the front pocket. At the top." His voice was tight, tense. She frowned as she fished around in the pocket. When her fingertips touched something, she grabbed hold and pulled it out without thinking.

"Yeah, I found..." she stared at foil squares containing condoms held in her hand. "Holy shit."

"What?" She heard voices, and remembered he had a final meeting with the city council today. "Sara, did you find it?" Her ears buzzed as she reached back into the recesses of the case and found his driver's license.

"Yes." She sat, and let the room narrow as her heart pounded so loud she was ready to make a 911 call for herself.

"Thank God. I've been scrambling around for it all morning. Sorry babe. Thanks for going back to the house for it."

She let him talk as she stared hard at the evidence of her humiliation. Gripped them, letting their crinkly noise fill her ears and cover the building hum of fury. She couldn't form words.

"Sara? Baby? You there?"

"Yeah. I'll put it on the kitchen counter. I'll be late tonight. Meeting Blake for dinner." She quickly made up plans, knowing if she said anything more it would come out in a primal scream of sheer outrage. "Bye." She let the handful of incriminating latex slip from her hands and hit the floor as tears blinded her vision.

Since getting engaged last fall, she hadn't gone more than twenty-four hours without talking to him, either by phone or by text, when they were apart. The level of control he wanted over her, the connection they shared since first meeting nearly a year ago, demanded it somehow. When he'd disappeared onto that plane for the convention in Las Vegas, it had felt as if he'd gone into a black hole.

The five days of "radio silence" had made her insane, first with anger, then fear, and then had circled back to bright red indignation by the time he got home. She'd stayed at his house for the first two nights, and then decamped back to her own neglected condo, unwilling to talk to anyone, not even her brother who'd banged on her door after she had ignored his calls for an entire day.

It had given her a clear glimpse into her future and she had zero desire to live through anything like it again. She knew should trust him. He'd told her many times, she could. The complete silence from him as he "worked" in a place she knew he'd be sorely tempted on many levels had built in her until she'd nearly exploded from the stress. Then he'd arrived, fresh faced, only slightly reeking of old booze and cigars, and she'd welcomed him home, relieved beyond measure to see him again. And now…

She stared at the phone that had started buzzing in her other hand. Blake. She wiped her eyes and answered it. "Hey. Can you meet me for dinner? I need," She stopped, unwilling to give anything away as her voice broke.

"Sure. What time?"

Relieved beyond words that he didn't ask what was wrong, she blurted out without thinking. "What the hell is wrong with me?"

"Nothing that I know of, other than a serious bout of poor judgment lately. But that's an argument I know I'll lose." He kept his voice easy, light, but she knew he'd picked up on her unhappiness. She bit her lip. "So…what time?"

The pub buzzed with activity by the time she walked in, her mind clear for a change. She'd used the entire busy day avoiding Jack's calls and texts and had reached the conclusion that she'd overreacted.

Who knew how long those condoms had been in there anyway?

She smiled when she spotted Blake's face behind the bar as he flirted with the many women sipping beer and giving him their full attention. Pocketing her phone, after reminding her fiancé that she had plans for the evening with her brother, she watched as Rob exited the kitchen, tension etched onto his handsome face.

"Blake!" Her brother glanced up from his extreme attention to a couple of very attractive women and frowned at his partner. "An alarm is going off in the brewery. Can you please handle it?"

Sara narrowed her eyes at the look of frustration Rob shot him. "I'll be right back," Blake patted her hand as he passed. She sipped the beer the bartender put in front of her, observing the two men and the palpable tension between them as they made their way back into the recesses of the huge building behind the restaurant. Within twenty minutes, her brother was back and perched on a barstool next to her, his green eyes clouded with something Sara realized was likely reflected in hers. She sighed and put an arm around him, kissed his rough cheek.

"We are quite the pair, aren't we?"

"Don't know what you're talking about." He kept glancing to the kitchen door, but it remained devoid of the tall, broad, blond man Sara knew he wanted to see. "So, what's the issue?"

"Oh, it's nothing, really." She picked at the salad she'd ordered, suddenly afraid to admit what she'd found or that she was willing to let it go. Her eyes felt hot, tired, and she glanced over at him. Blake stared hard at her.

"What the fuck has he done now?"

"I found condoms in his suitcase. The one he took to Vegas. The week he…"

"The week he made you a basket-case by not calling and talking to you at all. Huh. Imagine."

Anger flared in her chest. Her sudden desire to defend Jack nearly made her as mad as Blake's asshole-ish reaction to her dilemma. "Never mind." She sipped her beer and studiously ignored him.

"You're really willing to live like this Sara?" Blake kept his voice low but she sensed his tension mount as Rob made his way from the kitchen and took up a spot behind the bar, picking up the flirtation where Blake had left off with the gaggle of women at the other end. "I mean, did you and I not live through this sort of shit already?"

"What are you talking about?" But she knew exactly what he meant. Her face flushed and her ears started buzzing again.

She flinched when Blake put an arm around her shoulders. "I'm sorry." He sighed and kissed her hair. "I don't mean to point out the obvious." Wiping at her eyes before the tears could flow, she shrugged him off.

"Forget it. I'm sure it's…" She slumped; her earlier resolution, to let her anger at Jack go, to accept what was no doubt a perfectly decent explanation about his using the suitcase during an earlier trip, one he took before committing to her, faded. She had to believe that. It was that or drive herself completely insane thinking up all of the other reasons for him to have the stupid things.

"Don't make me say it Sara."

"Say what?" She pushed her half-eaten food away and propped her chin on her hands. Rob made his way down to them, leaned over the bar and brushed her cheek with a light kiss.

Blake ignored him. "That the guy is exactly like our father."

She closed her eyes. That concept had swirled in her head for weeks and since the utterly dreadful dinner she'd endured, when her high-powered fiancé had finally met her aging Alpha-male father, had become a clanging gong of fear.

"Blake," Rob's voice stayed soft but Sara heard the firm command of it. "I don't think…"

Blake's face reddened, and he startled her with his vehement response to his lover. "You don't know. That's the problem here. She's my sister. I don't care how long you've known the guy. He is not your family. You don't owe him anything."

Sara put her hand on Blake's leg, alarmed at the waves of unhappiness rolling off him towards the man she knew he loved. He glared at it, so she took it back. "Stay the fuck out of it," he ground out making Rob blink once, then walk away without a word.

"Jesus, honey. That was a little harsh." She stammered. She'd never seen them like this before. "What is going on with…?"

"*You* stay the fuck out of that, too." He kept his gaze trained down at the bar, then looked up at her, the bright green of his eyes shimmering with emotion. "I mean it."

She nodded, unable to form words in the face of her calm, stable brother's outburst. "Damn we suck at this don't we?" She picked up her beer.

"At what?" Blake slammed his and signaled for another. She sighed and leaned into his shoulder, comforted once again by his presence. He put an arm back around her. "Whatever, you do this at your peril." He picked up her left hand, and touched the huge diamond Jack had given her. "Seriously. You should know better. Don't let him get away with that bullshit now or you are in for the same life our mother lived."

Sara sat up and stared at him, relieved but furious that he'd put into words what had spun through her brain for weeks. Unable to muster indignation in the face of his obvious agony and relationship issues, she nodded, finished her beer and stood. "I gotta go."

"Tell him Sara. Tonight. Make him answer to you, and don't take a bullshit story."

"Fine. But you listen to me a minute." He shrugged but she pulled his face around to hers, pinching his cheeks just as he always did to get her attention. "You fuck it up with that man," she pointed to the kitchen. "And I never listen to a word you say ever again. Go back there and make nice. I mean it. At least one of us deserves to be happy."

Her brother's derisive snort before he sucked back half a beer did not make her feel any better at all as she made her way out the door, to her car, and towards the confrontation that had been way too long coming.

CHAPTER THREE

"It's over." Sara's voice broke the silence.

She slipped off the heavy platinum and diamond ring. Funny, the things a woman got used to. She'd never worn rings, but had immediately become accustomed to its weight on her finger. Her eyes stayed dry, but her heart kept breaking.

Jack stared at her as if she'd just asked him to eat his own gonads. He had been in the process of piling his wallet, Rolex and Mont Blanc in their usual, tidy spot on the hall table.

Sara had been waiting nearly two hours as she paced his tastefully decorated Art Deco style home from one end to the other, musing over the fact they'd christened nearly every single room in the place with various stages of sex. He loved foreplay on the massive leather sofa in front of the television. She liked it in the kitchen and in the spare bedroom they'd come to call their playroom.

A particularly intense session spent in his office, as she distracted him from his new construction project's spreadsheets. Sara sighed, her chest tight with anticipated loss. It was not healthy. Not anymore. Not if he wouldn't actually communicate with her beyond work or sex. Especially not now that she'd found the evidence of the essential truth about him. He would never change. He *was* her father. And she had zero interest in living the life her mother had, successful at work, yet seemingly unable to break from a poisonous relationship in spite of it all.

No thank you.

"What the hell are you talking about?" He ran a hand through his hair. His face looked tired; eyes glinted with something approaching anger. "I went out to dinner last month didn't I? Behaved myself? Let your asshole father make digs all night long about 'salesmen'? Christ."

He sunk into a chair across from her, elbows on his knees. Sara swallowed hard again. Edible-looking in her favorite suit, he remained an impossibility for her. He would not bring her happiness. Still, she had to clamp down on her sudden desire to say "Psyche!" and launch herself at him, then let him fuck her silly, again. Her hands shook. She clasped them tighter in her lap, her left ring finger bare and cold. The large ring glinted on the table between them.

"I know. And thanks. I just don't think it's going to work. I don't think..." The tears she'd held back spilled down her cheeks. Reaching into her pocket, she clutched the packet of condoms she'd discovered in his suitcase. The one he'd just brought back last weekend.

She tossed the packets of Trojans onto the table beside her discarded engagement ring. He stared at them, then up at her, confusion in his eyes. "What the fuck? Where did those come from?"

He kept a supply in his bedside table. They'd dipped into them enough in the past months, until the moment they'd stopped using them in St. Bart's. Sara closed her eyes, mentally counting the days since her last period.

"In your suitcase. You know, the one you just brought home. The one you asked me to look through for your ID?" It took all she had to keep her teeth from chattering.

His frown deepened. Then his eyes lit up. "Oh, babe. Those are from, oh shit, I didn't. Wow. This looks bad doesn't it?" He stood and walked to her, his presence sucking her in, making her want to forgive. But she wouldn't. Not anymore.

"Yeah, kinda." She rose to her feet and kept distance between them. He tried to get closer. Sara held a hand up. "Stop. Don't. I can't." She turned away from him, furious at her lame, girlie need to cry.

"Sara, I swear to you, those aren't from Vegas. Shit." He walked over to the liquor cabinet and splashed bourbon into a glass. "I don't know how long ago I used that suitcase. It's been over a year, I swear. You know me. I wouldn't have gone without...not back then...oh fucking hell." He sat back down. "You're right."

She whirled on him. More than anything in the universe, she did not want to be "right" at that moment. Part of her had counted on him to convince her otherwise; needed him to talk her down off the emotional ledge as only he could. A band tightened around her chest, making it frighteningly difficult to breathe.

She gulped in air, watched him put his hand in his hands. When he looked up at her, the "Old Jack" had fallen into place. The arrogant, fuck-the-world look fixed firmly on his handsome face. Sara had no faith in her knees to hold her. She gripped the back of a tall leather chair.

"I'm not good for you. Your brother, and no doubt your father, is absolutely correct. I'm a shit. I can't do this. I thought I wanted it, but." he downed the bourbon in one gulp, stood, and poured another, his back to her. She took a tentative step towards him, her hand out to touch his shoulder, when he turned to her. The look of extreme asshole replaced for a brief second with sheer agony. A sob tore from her throat. It was over. Ignoring his outstretched hand, she stumbled her way to the large front door.

He didn't try to stop her, didn't even call out. As if she had known where this headed using some internal failure radar, she'd already moved the few things she'd kept here back to her place. She stomped down the steps from the bungalow's large porch, ignored the swing they'd sat in just a week before and sat, drinking wine, actually discussing the wedding without him getting antsy and pissy. That might as well have been a million years ago. The stone that replaced Sara's heart sank further as she slid into her BMW, turned the key and pulled out his driveway for the last time.

The Indian summer heat baked her, but she rolled down all the windows, needing the fresh air, needing a reason to breathe. She'd watched him with her father, had seen him full on and had no choice. Her own mother had put up with a man just like Jack her entire married life. It had been brutal on everyone in the house. And Sara had gone and fallen for–shit, she'd nearly married–a man just like Dr. Matthew Thornton.

Sara shuddered not knowing if it was from fear or the anticipation of long nights of second-guessing she had ahead; or from the agony in her chest at thought of never seeing him again, never feeling his lips on hers.

She touched the phone button on her steering wheel. "Call Blake."

"What's up?"

She couldn't speak. Why had she called him anyway? So he could gloat?

"Are you okay? What did he...?"

"I gave him the ring back."

A solid minute of silence filled the car. Sara pulled into the parking lot of her condo community and put her forehead against the steering wheel.

"I'm so sorry Sara." Blake's soft voice made her want to strangle somebody, throw something that would shatter and do a ton of damage. "Do you want to come over?"

"No. I just thought you might like to know."

"Oh hell. I never thought,"

"Bullshit Blake. You never wanted this for me. You practically shoved me into this breakup. You know what, though? It's fine. You're right. It won't work. You knew it. Now I know it and I did what I had to do. But don't think I like it, because I fucking do not. I don't like it at all. I miss him already and it damned well sucks." She jabbed the "end" button. Tears burned hot trails down her face as she launched herself out of the car and towards the door, seeing nothing and knowing even less, other than she'd just either thrown away the best thing to ever happen to her or narrowly escaped a life she'd sworn she'd never live.

Jack watched his now ex-fiancé screech out onto the quiet street, sipped his bourbon and relished its slow lubrication of the horror at what had just happened to him. He sank back into the chair and glared at the fucked up still life of the condom and ring together on the table.

"Happiness thwarted" he could call it, or even better, "In Which Jack is a Dumb Ass." The purple foil packets stacked next to the nearly twenty-thousand-dollar hunk of metal and compressed coal he'd put so much faith in just a few months ago. "God damn it." He swept the whole mess onto the floor. His usual method of instant spin, how to fix anything, abandoned him. He had nothing, remained a hollow shell, scraped clean, raw and pulsing like a six-foot five-inch exposed nerve ending.

The fucking condoms.

He'd left them there from over a year ago. From when he'd taken that crazy-ass blonde bitch of a client away for a weekend. The weekend she tried to convince him to marry her. But he'd already met Sara by then. So, he had fucked the woman six ways to Sunday then dropped her at her house, his mind and heart elsewhere.

Oh, the bitter irony of the situation did not escape him. Vegas had been fun, sure. He'd flirted like crazy and let some ladies buy him drinks but he went to bed alone, every single night, without a single qualm or regret. He hadn't talked to Sara that week, but he'd been busy, serving on countless panels and attending dozens of stupid glad-handing receptions. When he wasn't doing that he'd played Texas Hold 'em and lost his ass, but even that didn't bother him. He'd had his mind firmly fixed on the future. With Sara. He'd even entertained a pretty out-there fantasy of her beautiful body, swollen and full with their child.

"Oh fuck." His face and eyes burned. His throat closed up. The room spun. He had to get her back.

How? Was he even worthy?

No, he wasn't but he didn't care.

Jack stood, retrieved the expensive ring from the floor and set it on the front hall table with his other stuff. His heart clenched at the sight of it. Anger followed close on the heels of despair. The house echoed with silence. He knew what he needed. Picking up his smart phone he quick dialed his oldest friend, Suzanne.

"Hey Jack, what's up?"

"I need to talk."

"Where are you?" As the noise of her beer bar receded, he assumed she must have walked into the brewery.

"Home. But I'm coming over. You gonna be there?"

"Well, I wasn't, but I'll stick around." Silence spun out between them before she spoke again. "You did it, didn't you?"

Jack dragged a hand through his hair. He knew exactly what she meant. "Yeah. I did."

"Oh hell, Jack." The ensuing silence deafened him. He trusted Suzanne more than he trusted just about anyone, except her business partner, who currently had his honeymoon to distract him. "C'mon over you fucking idiot. I'll buy you a beer." Jack slumped against the wall, relieved to have somewhere to go, sick to his stomach and emptier than he'd ever felt in his entire life.

CHAPTER FOUR

Blake didn't have to stay, but he did, busying himself behind the bar, which annoyed the perfectly competent bartender he'd hired. He was aware of Rob's voice in the kitchen, raised in increasingly louder decibels of anger. By the time the last customer had closed out their tab he'd run out of busy work and sat, nursing a dark stout beer and wondering where his relationship was headed. Rob had been his anchor for the last four years, his lover, business partner, closest confidant, and best friend. But the past months had been tense, to say the least. His chest constricted at the thought of losing the man.

"So," Blake started at the touch of Rob's hands on his shoulders and the sound of his deep, familiar voice. "How did it go at the bank?" Blake shut his eyes and leaned back into the other man's hands, letting him rub some of the tension out of his neck.

"About like you'd expect. But I think they'll give us the loan after we jump through a few more hoops."

"You understand how I feel about this." Rob kept his tone light, but Blake knew the undercurrent of disapproval well.

"Yeah. But if we want to distribute the beer,"

"Which, I don't think we need to do. Not yet."

"I know," Blake sighed. "Can we not talk about this tonight?"

"Sure. The silence that curled around them as the last employees shouted goodnight was anything but comfortable.

The bar manager approached them. A perky young female grad student, she'd brought a new level of organization to the place that Blake knew had helped. She was damn hot too. He stared at her a minute, taking in the curve of her hips, the swell of her breasts under the tight company tee shirt. "Hey guys. Um, you want me to leave the taps on awhile? I gotta go."

"Hot date Gwen?" Rob walked around behind the bar and poured himself a deep amber brew. "Lucky guy." He raised his glass to her, making Blake wince with realization that the man had been checking her out as intently as he had. "Go ahead and switch 'em off. We're headed out soon."

Blake watched her go. He couldn't help it. A woman's body was a wonder to him, always had been. He looked over to see Rob's eyes trained on the departing girl's ass as well. He met Blake's eyes and grinned, drawing a smile from him.

"You have to stop controlling your sister." Rob made his way from behind the bar, set his beer down and resumed his position behind Blake, putting strong arms around his shoulders, pressing lips to his neck. Blake closed his eyes, let his body react but his brain would not calm. He sighed and shrugged the other man off; cursing himself for being such a dramatic shit head.

"Whatever."Rob, ever the patient, calm one, took a seat and resumed drinking his nightcap. "You know what?" He kept his eyes straight ahead, mirroring Blake's stubborn avoidance. When the other man didn't answer, he went on. "You are really at risk of alienating her. Making the woman dread asking for your advice or help. She's engaged for Christ's sake. She said yes to him. Let them sort out their own shit. It's what grownups do."

"Huh," Blake turned to face the incredibly handsome man who'd rescued him from himself that day in Chicago. The weekend after Suzanne had dumped him with no warning, leaving him wandering the streets of a major beer festival in a daze. Rob tilted his head, waiting for Blake to continue. "Actually, they are not engaged. Not anymore."

Rob frowned at him.

"Yeah. Your pal Mr. Gordon, has remained true to form one time too many it seems."

"What happened?

Blake told him, keeping his voice neutral, trying to control the warring emotions of pleasure that it was over between his sister and that asshole, and deep sadness from the sound of her voice earlier on the phone. She loved the guy. He knew it. But this was for the best.

"Wow. No chance for explanation, eh? No opportunity for '*my pal*' to…"

Blake held up a hand. "No more excuses for him Rob. He won't change. Sara and I know his type, okay. I've explained it to you before. Our father…"

Rob stood, anger snapping in his eyes, startling Blake. "Jack Gordon is not your father, for God's sake. But, you've painted him with that brush now. I guess he truly has no chance."

"Hey, you don't know how hard it was…"

"Oh for fuck's sake, Blake. We all had our own dealings with dysfunction. Your mother seems perfectly content with her life now. You said yourself Matt quit fucking around after…"

"You don't know what you're talking about." Blake stood, meeting Rob's eyes, their bodies mere inches apart. He fought the extreme urge to kiss the other man, apologize, and just admit he was right. The minute he'd heard Sara's last words on the phone something in him wanted to tell her to take it back–to let Jack explain. He hadn't. When his lover pressed a hand to his face Blake closed his eyes, leaned into it a second, then moved away. "I'll be in the brewery. Need to check a few things."

"You have got to stop walking away from me Blake." He stopped in the doorway separating the restaurant from the brewery, his brewery, the one that had provided him the impetus he needed to get over the one woman he'd loved. The man who'd done just as much towards that end spoke words that sent a knife through

Blake's heart. "Or one of these days I won't be here when you decide to communicate."

He kept walking, let the sounds, smells and feel of the one space where he felt truly happy these days envelop him, shutting out the scary noises in his head that warned him he could be throwing away everything he loved, just because he felt so strongly about his sister's fiancé.

Noting the late hour, Blake realized he ought to be tired. He'd been up at five a.m. for a punishing workout, after which he spent two stressful hours across from a lender on a task he was foisting on his partner, he should have been exhausted. Trying to prove his worth, needing to see his products on store shelves and not just in the restaurant. Something else Rob was most likely correct about–but Blake refused to acknowledge it. Then he'd proceeded on to his usual ten hours of brewery work. His skin still crawled as if covered in ants. His brain hummed with a strange energy and his hands shook as he held a clipboard and tried to focus on the graphs indicating temperature changes in the fermenter in front of him.

"Fuck!" He heaved the board against the wall, and it made a satisfying clatter splitting apart and sending chunks of metal and molded plastic as it flew across the room. He put his hands against the cool stainless steel. Closing his burning eyes, he pictured her, her deep red hair, infectious smile, the woman who'd given him a chance as a brewer, taken his heart in her hands and then squashed it like a fucking bug.

"Calm down." Rob's voice in his ear, the sudden sensation of the man's body pressed against his back made him nearly leap out of his skin. "Shhh…It's okay. You're gonna give yourself an aneurism. Then I'd have to kill you for dying on me." Blake took a deep breath as Rob put his hands over the ones he had pressed against the fermenter, threading long fingers through his. His lover's lips at his ear, then his neck brought his cock to immediate attention, making him groan with the pain of keeping it trapped behind his zipper. A need so strong roared up from the soles of his feet, making the room darken, and then get suddenly bright.

"I need you," he could barely hear his own voice. "Please, Rob."

"I know," the other man soothed, keeping his lips against Blake's skin. Blake leaned his head against Rob's shoulder, arched his back and pressed his body even closer against his partner. Rob released one hand, keeping the other one tightly clasped in Blake's, pressed against the cold metal of the brewing vessel. Blake sighed as his lover stroked his rock hard shaft through his jeans, ran his hand down Blake's thigh and back up, cupping his need, never stopping the trail of kisses down his neck.

"Are we alone in here?" Rob's voice was breathy, rough with lust. Blake nodded. "Cause I'm gonna fuck you baby. You want that? I know I do." Blake felt his chest loosen, sensed his own pure need for everything about his lover pour through his psyche.

"I love you." He whispered, as Rob unzipped him, releasing his already weeping cock to the cool air. "Oh God," he groaned as the man passed a hand up and down his length, over the aching head of him.

"I love you too." Rob's voice anchored him, held him to the earth. Blake's natural tendency to lose control, the side of him he held tight around Sara so he could be what she needed from him, he'd only shown to two people: The woman who'd broken his heart, and the man who was gripping his jaw, turning his face around so their lips could meet.

Blake turned all the way around, needing the full contact, wanting to put his arms around his tall blond lover. Rob pressed into him, keeping his hand on Blake's cock, shoved his tongue between his lips, sweeping into his mouth as if he owned it. Their groans filled the room, as Blake threaded his fingers through Rob's thick hair and the other man increased his speed, using Blake's own fluid as the perfect lubricant. He broke away, staring deep into Blake's soul. "Let her go." He demanded. Blake nodded, more than a little confused as to who Rob meant until he realized he meant both of them. Let his sister live her life. Let go, once and for all, of the redheaded brewery owner who'd nearly killed him.

"Okay. I promise." He sighed as Rob turned him back around. He would do anything to keep the man in his life.

"Huh, not likely." Rob eased his jeans down and Blake stepped out of them, planning his feet apart, his hands back on the

stainless steel vessel in front of him. "I know you Blake Thornton.
Better than anyone. I know how your mind works." Blake felt the
other man's thick shaft against his ass, his strong hands gripping his
shoulders, trailing down to his waist and hips. "But it's okay." His
voice dipped lower as he positioned himself behind Blake.

Blake groaned as his lover touched a cum-slickened
fingertip against his ass, pressing in, breaching the tight ring of
muscles. "Let go Blake. I'm here. I'm not going anywhere because I
know you, and I still love you." He shoved in deeper bringing a
loud grown to Blake's lips, making him arch his back, offer himself
to the man. Rob shoved his tee shirt up, pressed lips to his back,
licked up to his neck, then bit down hard as he pulled out his finger
and pressed his cock into Blake's body with a hiss and a soft moan.
"Oh God. You feel so good."

Blake braced himself, letting his body accept his lover's
invasion, going beyond the pain and reaching the extreme pleasure
as Rob's long cock reached deep, caressing his gland. His own cock
jerked, leaked more and he closed his eyes, trying to do what Rob
said–trying to let go, to fall and let someone catch him. The smell of
their mutual lust swirled around him, the feel of his man's body
against and inside his and his own deep need for it all made him
gasp. When Rob gripped his hips and eased out and back in he
grabbed his own cock with one hand, keeping himself braced
against the vessel with the other.

"Harder," he grunted. "I know you want to. Take me like
you want." Rob groaned, dug his fingers into Blake's hips and
pounded into him. He felt the other man's intensity, his need to
prove something and he pressed back, pumping his fist against his
own cock as the orgasm gripped him, deep and Rob's cock pressed
up against his prostate, making him cry out and cover his hand and
belly with his own fluid. His body jerked and his brain continued to
buzz when he felt Rob change his angle and the speed of his thrusts.
With a grunt, Rob released inside him.

"Dear God, what you do to me," Rob draped across Blake's
back, wrapped strong arms around his waist, keeping their bodies
joined. Blake reached back and laced his fingers through his lover's
hair as his own body calmed, finally after the last two days of sheer
stress. "I'm sorry." Blake felt tears prick the back of his eyes.

"No." He stood, wincing slightly as Rob's cock slipped out of his ass. "You have no reason to be." He pulled his jeans up, wiped his hand on a nearby towel and turned, smiling, watching as his lover caught his breath, hands on hips. He tugged the other man's jeans back up, and then held his face between his hands. "I'm sorry. You are the best thing that ever happened to me. And you're right."

Rob raised an eyebrow, but returned his kiss, his lips firm and blessedly reassuring to Blake's orgasm fuzzy brain. "Hold on, let me get that on tape."

Blake pulled away, started to speak but Rob put a hand over his mouth. "No talking. Let's go home." He brushed Blake's lips once more then draped his arm over his shoulders and guided him out of the brewery.

CHAPTER FIVE

The sunlight pierced the blinds and stabbed Jack right between the eyes. He groaned and rolled over, right onto the floor. He played downward facing dog for a minute, getting his bearings, realizing this was not his expensive, imported carpet beneath his hands and knees.

What the hell?

"Jack?" a female voice called from the kitchen. He scrambled to his feet, looked down at his rumpled jeans and plain white t-shirt and took deep breath. He touched his denim-clad cock – morning hard, like a rock, and ready for action. He gulped.

Shit. Did I? Please God no.

He dropped onto the couch in relief when Suzanne emerged, two steaming hot mugs of coffee in hand. Dressed in her usual boxers and t-shirt, she curled her small frame onto the chair nearest him and handed over the cup. "So, you ready to talk now? Last night was more about showing off, wouldn't you say?"

"I don't want to know." Jack's head pounded in time with his heart.

She chuckled into her cup, her deep red hair scraped back into a ponytail, her face bright and clean, and refreshingly familiar. "No. You're right. You don't. I'm not a hundred percent sure but would guess there are some photos of you that look fairly incriminating."

He groaned. "Fuck. Me."

Suzanne set her cup down and smiled at him. "No thanks. Been there; done that. Didn't work for us."

He grinned at her and let the caffeine work its usual magic. One of those women most comfortable in the company of men, Suzanne always had a way of setting him straight. Time spent with her in high school and college convinced him that she had to be one of the more amazing women on the planet.

They'd cleared the air early in their relationship. One weekend in college on a ski trip, they'd been on a poor man's junket, sharing a room between four of them. After far too many schnapps shots and a bit of pot, she'd ended up passed out next to him. When he woke, his cock hard in ways only a young man's could be, she'd grasped it, rolled on top of him and fucked his brains out while their friends stayed passed out on the other side of the room.

Jack ran a hand down his face.

"Yo. Earth to Gordon. Where the hell did you go?" She snapped her fingers in front of his face.

"Just strolling down memory lane a little," he raised his eyebrows at her. She raised her middle finger in return making him laugh, which made him wince in pain.

"Okay. So. How are you gonna fix this you dumbass?"

He rose and took her cup, made his way into the kitchen and poured them more coffee. "She's just so, I don't know, stubborn, amazing, frustrating, perfect. You know?" She glared at him. "Yeah, I know, I'm no better."

"Look Jack, you are a smart guy. Successful, but Sara isn't a walk in the park. I know. I know her brother pretty well." Jack grinned when his friend's creamy porcelain skin flushed bright red. He put a hand under her chin.

"God you're cute when you blush red as a lobster." She jerked her face away from him.

"Fuck you. Now listen. Seriously, Blake is hyper-protective of her, I know, but he does want her to be happy. Maybe you should talk to him?"

"Right. The guy would just as soon chop me in half with his fucking black-belt Kung Fu grip. He scares the living shit out of me." Suzanne sipped and looked away from him. "Sorry babe. I know it's tough for you." He watched her swallow and blink fast.

Jesus, way to go Gordon. Make your one friend mad.

"No, no, it's fine. I just can't get past the God damned irony of you, in love with Blake Thornton's sister. Jesus. Seriously."

He pulled his friend to her feet and gathered her in for a hug. She sighed and leaned into his chest. "You might want to check your Facebook page." He groaned.

"I hate that shit. Talk about a necessary evil."

"Yeah, well a few of your pretty new friends from last night probably have you posted on their walls, complete with tags."

"Great. In the meantime, thanks for letting me pass out here. Some other time I'll admit that I have no memory of getting here. Humor me and tell me how fucking fabulous I was for you." She pushed him away.

"Yeah, right. That's past us, dude, remember? Now, get the hell out of here and get Sara back. Or I will kill you."

Sara's skin pebbled in the cool air. The ropes made a pleasant creaking sound and felt solid against her wrists. She'd accepted how much enjoyment she got from being bound, but Jack had gone slowly. Trust was still such a tough thing for them both to breach. When the room went dark, the soft whisper of silk tied behind her head, she tried not to let her teeth chatter.

"Shh, my Sara. All is well." Jack's deep voice rumbled in her ear. His lips caressed her cheek, neck, fluttered over her lips. She didn't respond. Knew she wasn't supposed to, not yet. His hands trailed down her skin, bushed over her erect nipples, across her stomach and hips all the way down to her calves. "I've got you. You know I've got you." She nodded, moisture slicking the top of her thighs as he continued to caress, tease and massage her entire body. She never knew where his hands would land next. She loved it.

As his fingers grazed her clit, trailed down her lips, dipping in and out enough to make her squirm and her skin flush with inner heat, she bit down on the urge to thrust her hips into his hand. "Mmm hmm, lovely." His fingers entered her, slow, spreading her walls, reaching up to tease the g-spot he'd discovered and used to his advantage.

"Ahh…" She couldn't help it. The fingers stopped. All was quiet. She knew he'd left the room. He'd done it before. His lips reappeared at her breast, sucking hard on her nipple then roaming upwards to her neck, jaw, and then her mouth. Dear God the man was a class-A kisser. She sighed into his mouth, letting him work his magic, the creaking of the ropes a musical compliment to the soft sounds they made between them. Then, he was gone again.

Sara shifted, knowing he'd be back. After what felt like an hour, she took a chance. "Jack?" Silence descended. Her feet were freezing, and her shoulders had started to ache.

Where in the hell was he?

Strange sounds started trickling in, Feminine noises, but not from her. Shuffling, moaning, Jack's voice raised but unintelligible. Then the absolutely, unmistakable sound of a woman in the throes of a monster climax worthy of a porn movie. Sara gritted her teeth. "Jack?" The ropes burned her wrists; claustrophobia hovered on her horizon. "Get this blindfold off me! Where are you?"

Then, blinding light as the cover was ripped from her eyes. A tall, sultry brunette stood over her, eyes gleaming, hands on her hips as she surveyed Sara's prone and vulnerable position. "Nice work honey. Thanks for waiting your turn."

Sara squirmed. "Where's Jack?"

"Didn't you know? He can't be trusted. Don't even try Sara. Don't even try." Then the woman was gone, and Sara saw her, wrapped around the tall frame of the man she had loved once, had trusted, once. The sound of her own scream woke her up.

She sat, clutched blankets to her mouth, her wrists on fire with residual rope burn from a few weeks ago. Her left ring finger was empty. Tears trickled down her cheeks and she flopped back on her pillows.

Oh yeah. She'd given it back to him.

This weekend she had to face him again in front of everyone at the Stewart Realty Company Picnic.

Wonder if faking a case of Ebola would suffice for an excuse? She sighed and climbed out of bed.

After a scorching hot shower, take-out coffee and a deep breath, she entered her office, slipping in the back so she wouldn't have to face the inevitable gaggle of colleagues at the front. She fired up her computer stared at the screen. It glowed, sharing more than she wanted to know. Stupid Facebook. She should have known better. She'd spent two days hiding out, gathering her mental and emotional resources together so she could face the office, ready to admit that she'd failed to hang onto the hottest bachelor in the tri-state area. Then she would avoid all conversations with anyone about their ruined relationship for a few weeks.

Her scalp tingled as she clicked through a series of photos posted to Jack's wall, in various stages of mouth fucking a couple of girls who, if they were twenty-one, Sara would be the god damned Queen of England. She sighed and noted the date.

The same as the night she'd given him his ring back. Perfect.

"Now do you see? This was the right thing to do Sara. You don't want to live our mother's life, remember?" She could practically hear her brother's voice. The ever-present, hugely annoying tears spilled over again.

"Hey Sara!" Craig dropped into the chair by her desk. She tore her eyes away from the searing images on the computer screen to acknowledge him. They hadn't spoken much in the last few months, not since their near close encounter just before Jack's big proposal.

"Hey yourself. What's up?" He put his hands behind his head. Sara allowed herself a very brief moment of admiration then snapped back to the present. She would not be distracted, especially not by this guy. That was the last thing she needed. The distinct memory of his full lips on hers, all those months ago, floated through her brain. She forced herself to focus on his words.

"My band is playing tonight. Here in town. We could use a few warm bodies," he raised an eyebrow at her.

She grinned in spite of herself. A night out. There was a pleasant thought. She hadn't had one in nearly a month. It had taken two weeks for Jack to get the loud and clear that she had no desire to talk to him, to make up, to make out, or of any of the above. It had nearly ripped her guts out, but had to be done. She swallowed against the image of Jack's face. It would never fade it seemed.

He'd obviously moved on, of course as the company gossip machine had cranked up, to the max. Heather, the long tall exotic drink of water who'd had her claws in him before he'd bought Sara the ring, was back in the picture with a vengeance.

"Um, hey..." Craig leaned in and gripped her hands. Sara realized she had a death grip on her knees and he her eyes closed. "Sara. Let it go." She sucked in a long breath.

"Yeah. Sorry."

He released her hands.

"So, about that show?" His voice had deepened.

She smiled at him. His handsome face lit up as he brushed his always too long hair from his face. She needed this. A friend. She nodded. "Sure. I'll be there."

"Good." He stood, then to her utter shock he leaned in, brushed her lips with his and whispered. "I've missed you." By the time he walked away, whistling, hands in his wrinkled khakis she acknowledged that maybe, just maybe she'd survive this.

CHAPTER SIX

Greg and Jennifer Stewart were the second generation to run the most successful independently owned residential real estate brokerage in the area. They had grown the company far beyond what his parents had started, and treated their employees and agents well. Formal Christmas parties, always at a different venue, and the "Party at The Farm" held every September, marking the end of the craziest and busiest season, were annual events. Sara pulled up to the massive compound, found a parking spot and sat, trying to catch her breath at the thought of being around Jack again.

They'd been promised "entertainment" and instructed everyone to come dressed to "play games." The invitations had said each employee was going to be paired with someone else; either another agent or a spouse/significant-other, and the Stewart Olympics would commence at six p.m. sharp.

Sara had invited Blake to come with her. But he'd backed out at the last minute to tend bar when one of his employees failed to show up for work. He had kissed her forehead, given her a hard squeeze, and pep talk when she stopped by the pub and had gotten the bad news. Noting that he seemed calmer, and that things between him and Rob had settled, she'd shrugged and left.

She parked her car among all the other high-priced automobiles, and took note that neither Jack's Stingray nor his new

Escalade was anywhere to be seen. She pulled her contribution of homemade chocolate chip cookies out of the trunk and walked towards her colleagues and friends who all greeted her warmly. Val ran up to her with an ice-cold beer.

"Here babe, drink this now" she insisted, before guiding her towards the food tables.

Sara laughed over her shoulder at various friends "warming up" up for the amateur Olympics by chugging beers. Recalling the last time she'd been at The Farm, she was grateful for the Stewart's strict "no drinking and driving" policy and for the large house they equipped to handle the many folks who'd be sleeping over tonight.

She turned to Greg Stewart to hug him and thank him for hosting another fun event for them and immediately spotted Jack over his shoulder. He sat on a blanket under one of the hundred-year-old trees with Heather, feeding her a strawberry. Her body stiffened and Greg pulled her closer, whispering in her ear as he led her away.

"Of all my agents, you were the last one I thought would go down this road."

She allowed Greg to pass her off to Jennifer, who put her arm around Sara's shoulders and announced that as the month's top producer, Sara would be the one to match up the teams. Val and her office manager, Pam, stepped up to record the couples, which kept Jack out of Sara's line of vision.

She reached in repeatedly, calling out names of oddball pairings, before finally pulling out her own name. She grabbed one more slip of paper, not really thinking much as the quickly consumed beer and residual shock of seeing Jack with Heather had made her head spin.

She unfolded the piece of paper: "Jack Gordon," and heard a collective gasp. She shrugged and rolled her eyes, bringing nervous laughter from the crowd. Everybody knew their story by now. No use pretending.

Glancing up she caught Craig's deep brown gaze, completely focused on her. She allowed herself a moment to look back at him before breaking eye contact.

"Sara," Jack nodded at her as they stood together to listen to the rules and regs.

"Jack," she responded, as coolly as she could manage. Her entire body hummed with familiar energy, but she held it at bay, let the anger focus her.

They performed the necessary egg-and-spoon trial, three-legged race, and wheelbarrow relays. The fireman carry provided a little diversion and Sara knew he used it as an excuse to hold onto her a little longer than was completely necessary. When they reached the final events, Sara and Jack were well ahead of every other team. She had another beer at one point, which loosened her up and allowed her to enjoy his closeness and the heat of his skin. She caught him staring at her, his eyes squinting as if trying to figure her out, as she won the hula-hoop contest on behalf of their team.

The final two events involved food and only included the top five remaining teams. Sara and the other four women, each given apples, were told to hold it in their mouth while their partners ate as fast as they could for twenty seconds. The team with the most-eaten apple would be the winner.

Sara sighed, put the apple between her teeth and turned to Jack, who immediately placed both hands around her waist and pulled her closer to him, his legs slightly bent, his head tilted. She closed her eyes until she heard the hoots and whistles of the crowd. She snapped them open and caught Val's wide-open eyes and shaking head over Jack's lowered shoulder.

In spite of herself, she let her body respond, taking no small satisfaction in the fact that he turned her around so that his back faced the crowd to hide his tented shorts. The crowd continued to catcall, egging him on, as the timer dinged. They broke away from each other, the electricity snapping between them, a completely cored apple in her hand and juice dripping down their chins. Jack wiped his off, not taking his eyes from her, before reaching out to raise her hand over their heads in triumph. The crowd erupted with cheers.

He laughed but dizziness made Sara's gut clench from such intimate public contact with him. Hands pushed her into a chair for the final event. A quarter of a watermelon was placed between her knees. Jack knelt in front of her. Her thighs trembled. Someone gave her another beer, patted her on the shoulder then walked away.

Jack grinned up at her, seeming to enjoy her discomfort. She glared back at him, and happened to look up, straight into Craig's dark eyes. He was standing at the front of the crowd, not clapping, watching her with an intensity that brought a chill to her spine.

She looked back down at Jack. Anger flared in her chest, and she smiled at him in such a way that made him pause, only perceptible to her, as she knew his small facial nuances very well. He hesitated slightly before leaning over her lap in anticipation of the contest. She drained her bottle, held it out for someone to take and placed her hands on either side of her knees, keeping the watermelon in place, flexing the well-honed muscles in her legs.

"Bring it stud, if you can," she told him loud enough to be heard by the first two rows of spectators. The crowd gave a collective "ooohhhh" and a few of Jack's cronies yelled out: "you can tap that Jackie," and "eat it fast, Jack" some of the louder ones.

She raised her eyebrows at him as if to ask "What?" and sat forward, allowing him a view of the tops of her breasts through her tank top.

"If you can," she whispered to him, again before she leaned back, her hands behind her head.

The crowd erupted again, hooting and calling, and Sara no longer cared that she was playing out some fantasy scene in a lot of heads as Jack leaned in to start eating the melon between her knees. The timer dinged, and he began to lick, slowly, scooping up big bites, his eyes never leaving hers. She was mesmerized and royally pissed at his little performance. He closed his eyes and licked his lips once, which brought a fresh round of hooting from the crowd.

He buried his face in the melon then, and the crowd went nuts. She glanced up, slightly off kilter from the beer and the heat. Her anger escalated. Her legs trembled harder as the sticky watermelon juice oozed down either side of the fruit. She knew the entire company was laughing at her, allowing Jack to do this to her in public, humiliate her while his new gal pal watched from the shade tree. She watched as he lowered himself for another ridiculous eating session, confident they would win the gold medal.

The asshole was making a mockery of her. A mockery of what they once had. Her eyes narrowed and she brought both knees together, hard, against either side of his face, which broke the melon in half without much effort and caused him to wince in pain and jump to his feet.

"Fucking-A Sara," he yelled at her as the watermelon juice ran down her legs. She stood up, realized she confirmed the suspicions of anyone who was too dumb to realize what was going on between her and Jack and ran into the house.

Gasping by the time she got to the upstairs guest suite, she leaned over the sink to steady herself, and looked up into the mirror. Her hair had broken loose of its tie back, as usual, and haloed her flushed face. She leaned down again to splash some cold water on her face, and allowed it to drip down her tank top onto her chest.

Damn him anyway.

She winced, reliving the scene she had just made in front of people whose respect she craved. They already worshiped him as some sort of god of the boudoir and she had managed to confirm that, acting like a jealous teenager, or one of his deranged, jilted lovers–not the calm, cynical ex-fiancé persona she tried like hell to adopt. She took another scoop of the cool water, splashed it on her chest and neck, and closed her eyes. Forcing herself to calm her breathing, she wondered how in the hell she could sneak away from this debacle.

She looked up in the mirror and there was Jack, right over her shoulder. She yelped, and turned around, backed up into the edge of the vanity.

He stared at her hard and didn't speak for a minute. Then he looked down and shook his head, hands on his hips. She waited for a split second, and then attempted to move past him.

"Excuse me," she mumbled.

He grabbed her, and spun her around to face him, his lips just above hers. He took a deep breath. The agony of having him so near, again, made her want to weep with regret. When he leaned in close, she sucked in a breath.

"We were about to win, Sara," he ground out between his clenched teeth. She stared into the dark sapphire depths of his eyes. They reflected something Sara knew she'd find in her own. Without another word, he covered her mouth with his, seeking her, seeming to need more of her than she had ever given him.

She pushed back on his chest. The slight damp of his t-shirt under her hands made Sara want to rip it from him. But she let her brain lead.

"No, Jack, not this time." She made her way towards the closed bathroom door. He allowed her to reach it and take a single step into the hall before he pulled her back, and carried her unceremoniously into the adjoining bedroom. She started to protest, but his lips covered hers, cutting off noise and logic. The proximity and familiarity of his body so perfect she almost cried with the effort of not begging him to come back, to ruin her life all over again.

She gave in, her hands buried in his hair as she pulled his lips harder onto hers. He slammed the door shut with his foot behind them more or less in the faces of Val and Jennifer who had just made it to the top of the steps.

Without ceremony, he flung her onto the bed, climbed up between her legs, shoving her tank top up and snapping the front of her casual bra easily between his fingers, never missing a beat. He took one nipple in his mouth, then the other, tugging, sucking, pulling at them until she arched up, barely able to contain her need to have him near her, inside her, all over her.

His lips moved up to her neck and he bit down. She gasped, surprised, at her body's reaction. She wrapped both legs around his waist, begging for more of him. Of their own accord, her hands reached for him–his hair, his neck, his shoulders, his back, his ass, unable to get enough.

His lips reached hers again, and he resumed his urgent kiss, seeming to want to possess her completely. She sighed with pleasure at the familiar feel of his lips. He grabbed her wrists and held them down on the bed beside her head.

"Sara," he asked quietly, "tell me what you want from me."

She stared at him a minute, unable to translate the look he was giving her. His eyes were dark with desire, his teeth clenched as though trying to hold something back, wanting her to say something, something that would satisfy him.

"I want you Jack," she hissed at him. "All of you," she said as she wrenched her arms free to pull him closer. "Now," she demanded, meeting his deep blue gaze.

"Then why the fuck did you throw that ring back at me," he demanded.

She turned her face away.

"Because, we just, we can't. We'll kill each other. It won't work," she insisted. "This is all we know how to do. Neither of us can handle anything more." The tear that leaked from one eye belied her brave words. She would give anything to take back that moment, to let him explain the condoms, but she couldn't. He would hurt her eventually. She knew it.

Don't live our mother's life. He will only hurt you. He'll never change. She tried to close her mind to the words, but they spilled through her like water over a cliff, uncontrollable and wild.

He had worked her shorts down and off, and she could sense his cock near her, throbbing with need. He thrust inside her with no preamble. Her body was already dripping and ready, but he shocked her with his force as she stretched to accommodate him.

No finesse, nothing fancy, just pure mutual, primal need connected them. His eyes bored into her, questioning without words as he shoved in further.

"So this," he grunted. His teeth still clenched, as if wanting something from her he couldn't even name. "This is all you want from me?"

She was shocked at herself yet again, at her response to his roughness, but unable to stop herself, as if the entire set of games they had just played outside served as quirky foreplay.

She wrapped her legs around him tighter, and her pussy clutched at him, pulled in him further, not allowing him to fully withdraw as her answer. The angle of his cock and the depth he reached meant pure ecstasy. She could sense him brushing up against her g-spot and she bit down hard on his shoulder to hold back a yell that would have surely reached the ears of everyone downstairs in spite of the blaring music. Her body took over completely; seeming to need something from this man who'd ripped her world apart, but who would not leave her in peace.

"Christ, Sara, I," he moaned again, his thrusts harder and even more urgent, owning her, possessing her. She felt him let go, knew when he was on the edge. His body shuddered, eyes closed, until he opened them and glared at her and groaned, filling her as her own body spasmed around him.

He stayed still for a solid minute. His breath calmed as he remained hard inside her while her own body twitched and pulsed, milking him, possessing what it could of him. He pushed himself up on his hands and stared at her, the look on his face something Sara had never seen before. It was searching, almost questioning; dare she say–needy?

He started to speak, his breathing still ragged. "Sara, I… we…" he trailed off and hung his head down between his shoulders.

She reached up to pull him close for a kiss, when she heard a small voice from downstairs:

"Jack? Jack? Where are you? They're about to hand out the prizes."

He rolled off her, yanked his shorts back up, and ran his hands through his hair; seeming to regain control of himself and whatever emotion had shown itself mere seconds before.

"Yeah, Jack, you scurry back to your date, K?" She hissed at him as she pulled her shorts back on.

"You didn't answer me." His voice was low and on the verge of an outburst, she could tell.

"About what?" She kept it cool. Had to, as a self-protective measure.

He gripped her bicep hard, which forced her to look up at him. He stared deep into her eyes. She drew her last reserve of control and scoffed. "Oh, right. Yes, what do I want from you? Well, I think you gave it to me just now, no?"

They looked at each other for a several seconds, each waiting for the other to speak, or break eye contact.

"Jaaaaack?" she could hear Heather getting closer, coming up the stairs.

"Uh, hang on a minute babe,' he yelled out not taking his eyes off of Sara's. "I'll be right out—must have had a bad bite of guac or something."

Sara pulled her arm out of his grip.

"You don't know what you want from me either. You think you do. You think you can buy your way into a relationship with an obnoxious diamond, but you've already proven to me that you aren't capable of anything beyond that. So don't ask me questions you can't answer yourself." She gritted her teeth. "Trust, Jack. That's all I required. The ability to trust you. But you can't give that, can you?"

He let his arms hang at his sides, and watched her for a brief moment, then seemed to mentally shrug his shoulders, and reach back into himself for the good old Jack they all knew. "You think you know everything about me. But you don't. Don't flatter yourself." His gaze took a hard edge and her heart broke yet again.

"I'll tell you what, how about you **never** touch me again, how about that," she felt her voice rising in spite of her extreme embarrassment at the knowledge that they had been conspicuously absent from the party for the better part of thirty minutes now.

She used "New Sara's" aggressiveness to her advantage, determined to purge this guy from her system once and for all. She glared at him, daring him—wanting him—to deny this. To reach out, take her in his arms, kiss her and walk out of this room with her.

He hesitated for the briefest of moments, and then ran his tongue over his lips.

"Sure, Sara, it was good for a few laughs—I got to show you a bit of fun, and I'll admit I had some too, but..." he shrugged his shoulders and turned away from her. "Time for Jack to pick on someone his own size for a while, huh?" he indicated the door and the nearly six-foot sultry woman waiting for him.

Fury pounded in Sara's ears. She spoke without thinking. "You are the most arrogant dickhead to walk the planet, but I'm sure this is not news to you," she was yelling and didn't give two shits who heard her. "If you ever come near me again, I will fucking rip your balls off, do you get me?" She turned fast then glanced back. But he had resumed his bemused stare, one eyebrow raised at her behavior, as she flung the door open, shoved past their small audience including Heather who waited patiently–stupidly, Sara thought–on the landing.

She was vaguely aware of Craig standing by Val at the foot of the steps but tears blurred her vision and she was determined to get the hell away before she embarrassed herself any further.

Craig followed Sara out, determined not to give into the intense and overwhelming desire to flatten Jack Gordon with one punch. He needed to focus on her. Then he'd worry about how he'd handle that asshole. Or, more likely, Jack being himself would continue to work in Craig's favor.

"Sara, wait!"

She held up a hand and kept making her way through cars until she reached hers. He followed, not sure exactly what he'd say. There was no doubt that she did something to him, something he wasn't ready to identify, but he considered himself her friend and one who wanted to be there for her at that moment.

By the time he caught up to her, she'd spent a few seconds trying to wrench open her door, but the tears streaming down her face made that tough. He set aside fury at the man who had done this to her and touched her shoulder.

"Don't." She shrugged. "I mean, I just, oh shit." She put her forehead against the car door. Craig turned her around, pulled her into his arms. She sobbed, clutched at his shirt.

"Shh. It's okay."

"No, it's not. You are such a great guy and he's... he's a..."

"Don't make me say it."

She laughed and tilted her wet face up to his. Craig couldn't resist the urge to brush her tears away but swallowed hard against the need to kiss her. Not now. But soon, he promised himself. Soon.

"Can I drive you home?" She leaned into his chest again and nodded.

By the time they got to her place, the tears had stopped. "Want to come in?" She sniffled. "I mean, you know, just to talk?"

He hopped out and opened her door. "Let's just sit here a minute." He guided her down beside him on the step. There was no way he was going in there. He knew himself well enough to know that he'd be unable to keep from taking advantage of her vulnerable state. That was not what she needed.

She went inside and grabbed them a couple of beers. They sat in comfortable silence a while. When she leaned her head on his shoulder, he shifted and put an arm around her. He knew what she'd done in that spare bedroom today with that asshole, Gordon. The need to seek him out and pummel him, and the desire to carry Sara inside and make love to her, warred in him so hard he had to bite his tongue to keep from saying something idiotic.

She stood, stretching. He tried very, very hard not to stare at the muscles in her thighs and imagine her body under his, her lips, her hair in his hands. He stood and pulled her close, kissed the top of her head and started down the sidewalk towards his truck.

"Wait. I mean, can't you stay?"

"No. You get some rest. You know where to find me."

He waved, climbed into his truck and tried not to groan aloud at the ache behind his zipper. This was going to be tough. But he was determined to prove to her that he was the better man by not rushing her, which might kill him if one could die from blue balls. He smiled at the text from her.

"Thanks. You are a good friend."

He waited to text her back until he had parked and was in the elevator, headed up to the penthouse pool to swim, until the need in his belly abated. *"I know."*

CHAPTER SEVEN

Blake watched as Rob fired yet another kitchen manager. The woman was not taking it well, but Rob wasn't intimidated. The tall blonde man squared his shoulders and escorted her to the door, opened it and she stomped out. Blake sighed, and turned back into the small brewery that comprised the middle two thousand square feet of the brewpub they'd opened and operated successfully for three years, in spite of the annoyingly constant turnover of staff. This meant one thing to him: Rob was spending yet more time here than at home.

He did a quick check of pH levels in the water where he was about to concoct a fresh batch of their very popular India Pale Ale. The previous day's batch was fermenting nicely, if the bubbly bucket of yeast next to the tall stainless steel vessel was any indication. Blake pulled his phone out of his pocket and noted a couple of texts, one from Suzanne Baxter, former boss and lover; and one from Sara. He leaned back against the copper brew kettle and read Suzanne's missive about her friend Jack. Frowning, he deleted it, sighed, and then hit the call button. The sound of her voice made him smile.

"Hey," she sounded a little breathless. He knew how hard she worked to make her brewery a success. Her drive had cost the two of them a relationship, but in hindsight, that was probably for

51

the best. He gazed out over the expanse of the empty restaurant at Rob.

"Hey yourself. What's up?"

"I'm on a mission of mercy."

Blake rolled his eyes. "Save your breath. Jack's history."

"How did you know I was gonna talk about him?"

"Because, my love, I know you better than you know yourself."

Blake let the silence stretch out longer than was probably necessary. He jumped when Rob put a hand on his shoulder and raised his eyebrows at the phone. "Sorry, but you know what I mean."

"Fine. But listen, seriously, he," Blake cut her off. Remembering his promise to Rob about not meddling in Sara's life, he clenched his eyes shut as the familiar Jack Gordon-induced anger roiled in his gut at her words.

"He comes near my sister again, I will kill him." Rob frowned at him. Blake turned away, intent and unwilling to let his lover's opinion of the man, who he'd gladly cut off at the knees, sway him.

"Please, Blake we aren't in high school here. Sara's a grown woman."

"Well, okay maybe I won't kill him. Castration could be arranged. He hurt her Suze, bad. I'm not gonna let that happen again."

"Don't coddle her Blake. It's not good for either of you."

"I'm not coddling. I'm keeping her safe from predators."

Rob snorted and walked away from him. Blake felt his scalp tingle at the sight of the blonde Adonis he'd fallen so hard for, right after the woman on the other end of the phone had dumped him. He closed his eyes.

"Enough about Sara. How are you? How's the new bottling line? The new distributor? I saw the lager at Meijer. Nice placement."

She laughed, making him shiver with memory. "Nice diversion Thornton. Well played." She sighed and he could picture her messing with the ends of her hair, worrying her lower lip with her teeth. He swallowed hard and willed his cock to stay soft. Damn they had been good together. But, he was happier now.

"Yeah, I'm good at a lot of stuff. So tell Gordon you tried and failed as his ambassador. Leave it alone."

"Oh, okay. Can't blame a girl for trying?"

"No, but I can blame you for your choice in friends."

"Last time I checked Rob was Jack's friend too." Her voice was sharp. "You're too overprotective for your own good you know. You should leave it alone."

"You gave up the opportunity to have much to say about what I do a few years ago." He bit down on the urge to be crueler. He wanted to be her friend, really. But hearing her voice still seared his nerve endings and turned him into an asshole.

"Whatever. Sorry to bother you."

"Wait, Suze, I'm sorry."

"No, you made your point. Sorry to meddle."

"But…" he spoke into the dead air. She had hung up. He slumped against the glass wall, a hand over his eyes. Damn her, she did it to him every time.

"Relax." Rob's voice was in his ear, his hand on the back of Blake's neck. He looked up into the other man's deep brown eyes. This was whom he loved now. The bitter irony that his own sister had been engaged to Jack Gordon, one of Suzanne's and Rob's oldest friends, wasn't lost on him. The extreme relief that she'd come to her senses and cut the guy loose had been intense at first. It had evolved into something that allowed him to sleep at night. Screw Suzanne and Jack. He pulled Rob to him, his hand grazing the other man's rough jaw.

"I know something that will help me do just that." He growled and ran his tongue over Rob's full lips, his cock stiffening behind the brewery apron.

"Mmmm, tempting indeed," Rob caressed his lips with his tongue, grabbed his ass and pulled up against his taller body before letting him go with a nip on his lower lip. "But you and I have too much work to do, lover. Besides, you'd just be fucking me to get over hearing her voice again. I told you once before I don't play that way." Rob stepped back and Blake bit down on the retort. "By the way, I heard that my friend Jack is getting a stronger grip on his inner Dom. Kyle told me he's been down at the club again, with Evan, Julie…and Suzanne."

Blake narrowed his eyes. Kyle was Rob's former lover and owner of the hottest BDSM club in downtown Detroit. "Thought you might be interested." Blake tried not to stare at the tall blonde man who'd saved him from himself that week in Chicago. "Oh, don't worry; Jack's not playing with her. They're just friends."

Blake gasped and gripped the edge of the window as Rob turned and walked away from him, whistling, hands in pockets. *Shit*. The man was too astute for his own good. He closed his eyes, willed his body calm, and turned back to the long day of brewing and trying to forget the feel of Suzanne's body under his hands once again, the way the sound of her voice made him react every single damn time still. Hoping he hadn't spoiled the lovely reunion they'd been sharing for the past couple of weeks, he forced himself to focus on the many tasks at hand. But, by the time they headed home, the tense silence had taken on a life of its own and Blake knew he'd fucked it all up yet again.

Sara stared at her phone's screen, trying to decide if it was worth her time to return the three calls from a needy seller, or to ignore her and answer Craig's text. It had been nearly three weeks since the disaster at The Farm. He'd been easy-going, flirty, but in a harmless way at work, never coming on too strong. She found herself looking forward to work, to seeing him, hearing his laugh and knowing his eyes were always on her. Did her ego good, after the beating it had taken at Jack's hands.

She squeezed her eyes shut. *Jack. Dear God would she never be free of him?* He had effectively ignored her, other than to check in and make sure she wasn't pregnant from the last time they…she sighed. *Craig*. That's what she needed. His lovely, soothing presence, which didn't compel her to necessarily strip off her clothes and fuck him every time she saw him, but did make her happy on a different level.

"Hey." His soft southern drawl made her smile and lean back in her chair. "So, I was thinking that you owe me dinner."

"How do you figure that?" Her scalp tingled. Why not?

"Because I bought the Coneys, remember?" She frowned.

"Oh, yeah. Wow, that was, like another lifetime ago."

"Yep. So, what's on your agenda tonight?"

"Uh, tonight? Okay." She was free and, in fact, ready. Ready to take this a step further with him. Or at least try. "Meet you at The Local? Seven?"

"Your brother's place? Sure. See you then." She smiled and put her chin in her hand.

"I'm looking forward to it, Craig."

Sara breezed into The Local by six thirty, her last appointment having canceled on her, leaving her with an hour to spare. She grinned at the sight of her handsome brother, bossing the bar staff around. The jerk always was over protective, but she did love him.

He put an ice-cold martini in front of her as he finished chewing out some bartender for not cleaning glassware properly. She frowned. He seemed tense, not himself. But his familiar grin eased her nervousness as he leaned over the bar and pecked her on the end of her nose. "What's up sister?" He grabbed a clean towel and started fussing with the pilsner glasses.

"Oh, not much. Got a date." She did a quick smartphone email check. When she glanced back up at him the look in his eyes alarmed her. She turned to see what he was staring at. Rob was across the room, chatting and laughing with a couple seated at a table near the front window. She looked back at him, eyes narrowed. "What's wrong?"

He shrugged. "A date huh?" She sighed and let him create the diversion. He was not good at talking about himself. It had been a solid month after he had broken up with Suzanne before she even knew about it, which had pissed her off to no end. He'd worked there for another couple of weeks before heading to the Midwest Beer Festival in Chicago where he'd met Rob. God she hoped nothing was wrong between them. They were the one solid thing in her life. She let him putz around and ignore her a few more minutes as she sipped and tried not to be anxious about an actual date with the man who'd nearly seduced her the night before she'd accepted Jack's marriage proposal. Her skin prickled, as if the air conditioner had been cranked up. She swallowed, suddenly tense. When she looked over at Blake, he was frowning, hands on his hips. "Let me guess Sara," he jerked his chin at something behind her. "This date. It's not with Jack." She opened her mouth to talk but the sudden scent of him filled her nose.

"No." Her voice cracked. "It's not."

"Good."

The large familiar hand on her shoulder made her whole body zing like a too tight violin string.

"Hello Gordon. The usual?" Blake's voice was icy calm.

"Sure. Thanks." He took a seat next to Sara. She crossed her legs and kept as much distance between them as she could. If it were possible, he looked handsomer than ever. She sighed when he bumped against her shoulder playfully.

"Don't touch me." She drained her martini and set the glass down, but her voice was weak and she knew it. Visions of them in that open house, his commanding tone, the hallway the first time, she shut her eyes against the overwhelming compulsion to climb into his lap. Damn him.

"Sorry." He sipped the brown liquor in the rocks glass, keeping his eyes forward, mirroring her.

She sighed, determined to be an adult about this. "How's the city commission these days? Get that approval yet?"

"As a matter of fact, I did, just today and came in here to celebrate."

"Congratulations." She shut her eyes against the inner calendar that had been so prevalent in her life for so many months–the one that reminded her that, if she had not broken it off with him, she'd be marrying the compelling man sitting next to her about the time the new building would open. They made plans around it, in fact. "Shit."

"What's that?" He looked at her, his deep blue eyes concerned, making her look away.

Fuck him and his fake emotions. The sight of Craig entering the door, clad in ass-hugging dark jeans and what looked like the softest blue button down shirt in the universe hanging over the waistband in his typical, too-cool-to-be-sloppy way lifted her heart. Yes. This was why she was here. She stood.

"Nothing, sorry. I, um, gotta go." She waved at Blake. Before she could make her way over to him, Craig appeared at her side, hand stuck out to shake Jack's, whose eyes narrowed at the sight of them, standing close. Sara flinched when he put an unwelcome arm around her waist. *What was he playing at?*

"Gordon, congrats on the council meeting. Full steam ahead, eh?"

"Yeah." Jack shook his hand, never taking his eyes from Sara. She looked down on reflex, then back up at Craig as his arm tightened around her. "Thanks."

"Shall we?" he asked then turned her before she could say anything. She felt her face flush. The obvious pissing contest she'd just witnessed might have flattered another girl, but it aggravated her to no end. The last thing she wanted was to be some kind of trophy between these two men. She stepped away from Craig's arm. He smiled and pulled out her chair when they reached their table. She frowned at him, suddenly questioning her motivation for being here.

"Don't do that." She stared at the menu as they sat.

"Do what?"

"You know, poke a stick in a pit of vipers. Egg him on," she jerked her head to the side. Jack was still at the bar, and his stare was burning holes in her psyche. She glanced up and placed her drink order, took a deep breath and focused on the handsome man across from her. If this whole getting beyond Jack thing was going to pick up steam, she knew she had to give it a boot in the ass herself. It was the perfect night to do it.

But did she really want it? Her tingling scalp and still zinging nerve endings told her that her former fiancé still sat at the bar and those deep blue eyes trained right on her. She closed her eyes, then opened them again, and gave Craig a huge smile.

It took every ounce of Jack's inner reserve not to crush the glass in his fist as he watched that *kid* put a hand on Sara's back and guide her to a table. He tried not to watch as the smarmy little shit pulled out her chair, but his eyeballs would not cooperate. His jaw ached already from keeping it clenched nearly twenty-four-seven, ever since she had left and he'd been battling the city. He'd been pouring all his sexual energy into banging Heather's brains out for the last several weeks. He still twitched with a near constant dissatisfaction.

Shit.

He made himself ill. He wouldn't let his own sister within a country mile of someone like him. How could he blame Blake for "protecting" her? Christ. He perused his smartphone email inbox on autopilot; ignoring the near-constant stream of dirty texts from the woman he'd swear he'd called Sara at least once the night before. Sighing deeply, he looked up and straight into a pair of eyes as green as the woman in question. Instead of the usual raw hatred, there was pity in Blake Thornton's eyes as he pushed a fresh glass of bourbon across the bar.

"Thanks." He turned, not wanting anything resembling conversation with Sara's brother right now. He had never, in his entire life felt more torn or confused about what to do or how to act. He kept watching her, sipping his drink, flashes of memory shooting through his brain like daggers. How in the hell he'd messed this up so completely, he still wondered. Yes, it was in his nature. He couldn't be trusted, could he? Certainly, if his behavior recently with the eager Heather was any indication, "pining away" for the woman across the room from him, the one who had so captured his very soul, was obviously not on the agenda. He shot Heather a quick text:

"Not tonight. Too tired. Talk tomorrow."

"Jack!" He turned to see his old friend, Rob Freitag, walking his way. Rob had been a serious cohort in the deflowering of campus virgins back in their college days. The guy had swung both ways then too, but it hadn't been an issue for them. Women had fallen for their one-two punch; tall, blonde or dark, and charming, like leaves from a tree, once upon a time. He grinned.

"Pull up a chair. I could use a hard punch in the nose right now. You game?'

Rob shot an odd look towards Sara's brother, who stood at the other end of the long bar, staring at them. "Huh, might make two of us. I seem to have done a bit of screwing up a relationship with a member of the Thornton family myself."

Jack rolled his eyes and laughed as the other man eased himself into a barstool. His heart still pounded and spine tingled at being so close to Sara again, but unable to do anything but watch her laugh and lean into the surfer kid who kept reaching out to touch her arm, shoulder. Jack closed his eyes then refocused on Rob.

"Dude, you have no idea."

As the dinner progressed, Sara forced herself to be calm, to focus on Craig's dark brown eyes, to listen to his soft Southern drawl as he answered questions she didn't remember asking. She flinched when she felt his palm on her knee.

"Earth to Sara." His voice was soft. She sat back and pushed her plate away, no longer hungry. "You still there?"

She smiled at him, letting his smooth, handsome face and calm manner soothe her rattled nerves. "Sorry. Lame."

"Nah, long as you're buying, I'm good." He shot a look over to the bar. Sara wrestled her rapidly rising ire.

"Okay so I'm nipping this in the bud right now Robinson."

"What's that, dear?" He finished off his blue cheese burger and wiped his mouth. She found her eyes drawn to his lips, suddenly hypnotized by the memory of them on hers.

"The dick-measuring thing you're doing with my ex-fiancé over there, that's what. Cut the shit out."

He raised an eyebrow and put an arm over the back of his chair, letting his long legs stretch out to the side of their table. She suddenly relaxed as if he'd flipped a switch in her psyche. It was clear she had no business messing around with him, but there was a buzzing need in her brain that she knew, damn good and well, was the connection she shared with the man currently laughing his head off with her brother's lover. She also knew she had to find an outlet for it if she were to sever that connection with Jack once and for all. She leaned in on her elbows. He frowned at her.

"Then stop flirting with me. You're just as bad as he is." She sat up and glared at him. Familiar words, and ones she did not need to hear right now.

"I am not." His wide grin made her scalp tingle. "Okay, I am. But not for his benefit."

"Then let's get out of here." He leaned over and grabbed her hand, staring at her so hard that, for the first time in an hour, she forgot about the man across the room. "It's making me antsy with him over there, I won't kid you." He stood, held out a hand. "I'm sorry. I don't mean to, you know," he shrugged as she stared at him.

"Act like you're a dog who felt the need to piss on my leg?" He laughed at that, and hauled her to her feet, pressing her close.

"Yeah, I forgot for a minute to hide my inner dog from your inner bitch." She let him kiss her, just a light press of lips together before stepping away. "Let's get ice cream or something, a movie, I don't care, something so I can prove my good intentions." She smiled, and without a glance at the bar's direction, let him guide her out into the cooling fall evening.

As they walked past the bank of windows along the bar where Jack still sat, he grabbed her hand. "I don't share well Sara, I won't kid you. So when you're clear of him, I'd like to show you how a real man acts, but until then, ice cream is on me." She gasped when he put her hand to his lips, kissed it, and then kept his long fingers threaded through hers as they made their way down the street.

A sudden light went on in her head, spread its warmth down her spine and caught a slow burn as she watched the handsome young man flirt naturally with the girl dipping ice cream. She followed the line of his shoulders down to a trim waist, firm ass, and long legs and let herself imagine a moment, held by him, easing the ache in her body she should exorcise. Rid herself of Jack's hold on her for good. When he glanced at her, as sensing her stare, his eyes widened at her pointed look, then feigned a look over his shoulder before pointing his own chest.

She laughed, leaned in and planted her own kiss on his firm lips. "Yeah, you. You are too cute for your own damn good, you know?"

"Well, I've been told..." he handed her a cone towering with butter pecan, "But you'll have to find out for yourself I guess." He grinned, wiped a blob of cream from her nose and put his finger to his lips. She shivered.

Yes. This was the solution. She hoped. If not, she didn't know what she could do to get Jack out of her life, her head, and her heart. She sincerely hoped Craig wouldn't mind.

CHAPTER EIGHT

Sara shook her head to clear it as a familiar voice echoed through their office. She closed her eyes and rubbed her forehead, praying she could shove him out of her head and her office by the sheer force of the pressure. It had nearly six weeks since that party, and the damn man appeared nearly daily in her space. She looked up at him as he leaned against the doorway of her cubicle. He smiled, sending signals she could not control clanging around in her brain. She gritted her teeth and turned away.

"How are you feeling, Sara?" he asked, an innocuous comment meant for public consumption. "You don't look so good." He moved closer, his eyes changing, losing their cold glitter. Realizing what he was really asking, she straightened up in her chair, observing him, fascinated by his seeming interest in the current condition of her body.

"Hey, you lost your touch? You never tell a lady she's not looking too good." Sara tossed her hair back. "I'm fine maybe a little more tired than usual," she told him, unable to resist. "Can't figure it out, really, but I'm sure it's nothing." She turned to her desk, brain spinning, counting subconsciously, backwards from her last period.

Before she could finish her frenzied mental calculations, she sensed another male presence behind her, and groaned inwardly, wondering what the hell she had done to bring on this testosterone battle. Craig walked into her cubicle past Jack and leaned up against her desk. He addressed her, ignoring Jack completely.

"Hey, I hope you don't have plans for tonight." She looked up at him, surprised. They'd had a few pseudo-dates. She'd been to see his band a couple of times. Her plan of attack–to seduce him, get what she needed to shake her physical craving, had been thwarted time and again. He would not engage with her beyond friendly "buddy" status. Stubborn man.

"No. Not really," she told him, her voice weak, the tension between the two men nearly suffocating her.

"Good, I'll pick you up at your place, say, seven?" he leaned down and kissed her lips, softly, quickly. "Bring your swim suit," he whispered into her ear.

Craig walked out, nodding at Jack without speaking, which left her with her thoughts, wondering if she even had a presentable swimsuit, when she should have started her period. She was acutely aware when Jack quit staring at her when he turned and left the building without another word to anyone.

She hurried home at six, wondering what the hell Craig had planned. She found a sexy bikini and shoved it down in a bag, with a hairbrush and an extra set of clothes.

Craig rang the doorbell at seven sharp, and she walked out, the bag over her shoulder, having calculated that her period had appeared on schedule two weeks ago and so Mr. Gordon was off the hook.

He smiled at her, that lazy, relaxed way that caused her heart to flutter with renewed purpose. No, he didn't set off fireworks in her like Jack did. But that *was* the whole point. She decided to take the direct method. "Why does this feel awkward all of a sudden?" He glanced at her before starting the engine.

"What does?"

She swallowed hard. "Well, I've been trying to get in your pants for weeks now and you are either a virgin or I smell bad. So, I don't know where this is headed tonight, but I'm interested to find out."

He put a firm, possessive hand on her thigh. She stared at it. "So what is this about? You tell me." He leaned over then, pressed his lips to hers before she could answer, the hand now behind her neck, holding her close. The firm, gentle connection calmed her. None of the frantic need she had always had with Jack emerged, but that familiar slow burn ignited in her belly. One she recognized, and welcomed. She broke the kiss. His lovely brown eyes darkened as the silence swirled around them.

"I need this Craig. But I doubt I can offer much more than, well…" She pulled out of his embrace and stared straight ahead, hating the sound of her own voice. "I need you as a friend, but, um, sure could use some benefits. Does that make…mmph…?" She gasped when he yanked her close again over the console, owning her with a kiss that promised much more. She melted, threaded her fingers in his hair and let it take away the yawning emptiness she'd lived with for over a month.

When he released her, his breathing ragged, he pressed a kiss to her hand and tugged it down to his lap. She grinned at the hard heat under his zipper. "Is that a yes?"

He groaned, let go of her and squealed out of the parking lot. "You're impossible, you know that?" She giggled, the slow burn spreading, making her thighs tingle. She put a hand on his neck, laced fingers through his hair.

"No, I'm not. Just horny. So what?"

"Yeah," he laughed. "Me too."

They made their way downtown, and he pulled into the underground lot of a tall condo building. The elevator eased them up to the top floor and Sara allowed herself to admit how wrong this was, but that she could not wait to see what he had to offer.

The doors opened onto the top floor, revealing a glass canopy over a large blue pool. The entire place sparkled with candles. She gasped, and glared at Craig. "You were gonna do this anyway? And still made me say it?" The twinkle in his eye made her gulp. *God he was cute.* "What do we do when anyone else wants to swim?"

"I've lived here for nearly two years and I have never once encountered another soul in this pool, so I'm locking the door behind us." He showed her the changing room, and she put on her bikini, amused at his modesty. He stared at her as she entered the pool area again; dragging his eyes from her toes to the top of her head, then looked straight into her eyes.

"Wow," he said, softly.

She was just what he had been imaging for weeks—firm, fit, not too thin, her breasts a perfect match for her body type, her nipples rock hard under the thin material of her suit, and her skin glowing in the soft candlelight. He couldn't get enough of her, just the sight of her, her lower lip caught in her teeth… he smiled, forcing himself to stay calm, to keep his desire in check—for now.

He had his regular spandex trunks on and made no effort to hide the bulge there. It would have been impossible without a towel anyway. She ran her fingers over his shoulders, as if measuring him for a suit, lightly touched the skin of his biceps, forearms, wrists, and hands. He remained still for her, not moving or touching her, as her fingers lingered on his chest down to his abs.

She stepped back then, seeming to wait for him to make the first move. Something inside him snapped. He scooped her into his arms, reached his hands into her hair and kissed her, kissed her like he'd wanted to do for months, since the first time he'd seen her in that sales meeting. The soft noises she made nearly drove him insane, but he broke away, reminding himself to go slow. Stepping back, he took her hand and led her to the edge of the pool. Then, without another word turned and plunged in the deep end, rising to the surface to break through for breath, trying like hell to bury the lust and the "something else" burning a hole in his gut.

Sure he could be friends, fuck buddies, whatever. But he knew he would want more—a lot more. He didn't know if going down this particular road would be good for him in the long run. Tonight, he had no intention of holding back.

She watched, mesmerized by his lithe body as it cut through the water. When he resurfaced having completed a back and forth lap in no time, he grabbed her feet and forced her to the edge.

"Come on," he said, "let's see how in shape you really are!"

She squealed, embarrassed. Swimming had never been one of her favorite forms of exercise. Something in her wouldn't relax enough to feel comfortable with the water up her nose, pulling at her limbs, forcing her down while she struggled to remain afloat.

She jumped in and hung on to the side.

"You go ahead," she told him motioning for him to swim away. "I like watching you," she laughed. "I'm a terrible swimmer."

"I'll teach you," he said, running a hand through his hair.

She tensed up, almost told him this wasn't exactly the sort of "exercise" she had mind, but decided to humor him. He pried her fingers off the edge. "C'mon, I won't let you drown, jeez." When they got to a shallower spot, he took her wrists, formed her hands into cups. "Like this, push the water away from you with your hands." She shuddered when he pressed a kiss into each of her palms.

"Kicking keeps you buoyant, your hands and arms move you forward. Now show me." He pulled himself up with those amazing arms and sat on the side of the pool.

"Okay fine." She pushed off from the side, concentrating on propelling herself forward with her lower body, forcing her arms to move independently and to turn her head to the side at every other stroke to catch oxygen just as he'd taught her. Her brain went immediately into what she recognized as her zone, that place she retreated to after five miles of running or the first hour of hot yoga. She continued to stroke, kicking, breathing comfortably and not panicking as she had when she tried to swim laps before. She reached the side at Craig's feet and stopped.

"How's that coach?" she asked, smiling and batting her eyelashes.

Without a word, he walked around to the deep end again, motioning for her to follow him. She climbed out, feeling strong, relaxed, and happy.

He showed her how to dive in, bending down deeply first, and then holding her hips up, in preparation for the exertion.

"Okay, but I know you're using this as an excuse to touch my ass." She smiled then gasped as he yanked her back up and slanted lips over hers. He broke the kiss, keeping his arms around her waist. Her head buzzed and her core resumed its slow meltdown.

"Maybe, but it sounds like I don't need an excuse." He released her, smacked her ass so hard she yelped as he dove in. Her inner competitor reared up, and she followed him, hands and head first. She caught up with him, then turned around and swam back. She kept up for nearly six laps, then slowed, her heart pounding and her breath coming in gasps. Finally she stopped, clinging onto the side, watching as he slid back up to her. He smiled, placed his hands on either side of her arms, staying afloat by kicking his feet.

His face was near, his lips hovered over hers, his eyes closed, his breathing ragged. She sighed as he pressed her against the edge, the hard, lean planes of his bare body sliding against hers.

"Look up Sara," he whispered, sending shivers through her whole body.

Craig couldn't remember a time when he felt so alive. The steam from the pool, the familiar chlorine smells enveloped him as he moved closer to her. His pulse raced but he kept his movements slow, relaxed, determined, and ready to fulfill whatever she needed from him. He was winning this one, he knew. Jack Gordon would be a distant memory once he was through with her, maybe not tonight, but very soon.

No, she said it herself. Friends. With lovely benefits. He grinned, and yanked a mental pillow over the voice reminding him he was likely already halfway in love with the woman.

She tilted her head back then gasped as he put his lips on her collarbones, moved up her neck, and took her earlobe between his teeth. Her body arched into his.

"Is this a good idea?" She breathed into his ear.

He sighed, bent his head down to her bikini top, pulled it aside easily with his teeth, pulled a rock hard nipple into his mouth. His entire body pulsed when she moaned.

"Craig," Her hands were in his hair, threaded through the wet strands. "Are you sure? I mean, don't want to…oh dear God." He pressed against her, cutting off her protest with his lips and tongue. Her arms shook as they wrapped around his neck but broke their kiss. He stared at her. "I know you're right, what you said. I owe it to you to get him out of my system," she began as he pulled back and watched her brush the tears away.

"No," he said firmly. "You owe it to yourself to get him out of your system, and I've decided to dedicate every waking hour to helping you do just that."

Sara's brain slowly closed down as she gave into the burning need for something, anything, denying to herself that she could be using the incredible man in front of her to get over one who wasn't worth carrying his guitar case. He leaned in and took her lips, caressed them with his, explored her mouth with his tongue. She wrapped her legs around his waist, held on, felt his cock pulse under the thin trunks. He reached down to release one leg, and placed his entire hand against her pussy, rubbed through her bikini bottoms exerting just enough pressure against her mound with the heel of his hand.

"You game for that plan, Thornton?" He whispered, using his teeth to graze her skin along her jaw. "I mean, if you wanna think you're deflowering me you can, but you'll find me fairly talented for a beginner."

His incredibly fit swimmer's physique held them up as he plunged his tongue between her lips again. Her body arched, and she pressed herself down into his hand, willing him to reach inside, to fill her aching emptiness.

He reached around her waist, and down into the back of her swimsuit, feeling his way with his fingers, and touched her engorged clit, passed by her lips, and over her tightest hole before repeating the process, the entire time holding her up with his arm wrapped around her.

"Oh my God, Craig, please don't stop," she heard herself begging as her body started its slow, familiar dance towards orgasm. His lips remained on hers, not breaking contact, except to lean down and nibble at her neck. His lower body moved against her seeking contact. She gasped, and buried her hands in his wet hair, pulling him closer, feeling his fingers reach into her pussy, as light exploded behind her eyes. "Jesus, yes!" Her whole body pulsed, shivered, and tension she'd held for weeks released in a rush of lusty adrenaline.

He removed his lips from her neck, his eyes half closed, his nose flaring as he brought his fingers up to his lips to taste her. Then, without warning, he reached down to her waist and placed her up on the side of the pool.

He yanked her bikini bottom down, tossed them aside, never taking his eyes from her body, then reached around her ass with both hands and pulled her to his mouth, flicking her still sensitive clit with his tongue.

"Ahhh," Sara fisted her hands in his hair as he licked the tender nub, and spread her lips with the fingers of one hand. She bent one leg allowing him more access, willing him to take more of her.

"Oh God, Craig, yes, please, yes!" The room kept spinning and she couldn't stop coming. It amazed her, nearly bringing tears to her eyes. Finally, he eased his fingers out, pulled himself up out of the pool and stood over her. She eased back away from the edge of the pool, willing him to put his incredible body between her legs and fill her with that amazing looking cock. He continued to gaze down at her, the bulge in his trunks seeming to grow as ever larger. Suddenly, he knelt down.

"I told myself I would wait for you, as long as it took," Craig lowered his head briefly then looked straight into her eyes, boring into her soul. "I have never been so close to murder with my bare hands as I was the day of that damn picnic. It's probably not fair for me to say I'll just be your friend." He drew his fingers down her throat, to her breasts, cupped them gently, and trailed a line down to her navel, as if pondering her flesh, how it could possibly be here, in front of him, his for the taking. Then, wordlessly, he stood and walked over to a small table that held a bottle of wine, two glasses and a single condom.

He opened the square package, pulled off his trunks as he faced her, and her eyes were drawn to the beautiful sight of his cock as he drew the sheath down its length.

"That for me?" She licked her lips and smiled when he actually blushed.

He sat back on the side of the pool and slid into the water, and pulled her towards him again, easing her back down into the water with him. "Yes. It is. You sure you want it?" She wrapped her arms around his neck and buried her face in his shoulder, nibbling, licking, tasting water and sweat, the very essence of Craig. He pushed her against the side of the pool with his body, and she reached down to stroke him. He groaned and leaned into her pressure. "It might come with strings attached, no promises. Okay, Sara?" He tilted her face to his and covered her mouth, plundering her with his tongue. She broke away, wrapping both legs around his waist.

"Pretty sure, yeah," her voice was hoarse. She couldn't wait another minute to appreciate fully what he had to give and grasped his long and elegant cock in her hand. The water made her more buoyant, and she lowered her aching sex down his length, gasping as she felt length go ever deeper. "Dear God…" The sensation of his strong arms holding her up as he pressed in further brought stars to the edge of her vision. She moaned as he took her hips and eased her back up, then back down, slowly, steadily, his pubic bone making exquisite contact with her clit.

He grasped her around the waist and turned them around so that he was leaning against the wall, and she had her hands on the side of the pool, on either side of his shoulders. He took her face in his hands.

"Look at me Sara, now, please."

She opened her eyes, drank in his gaze, as his hips began to move against her, his lips found hers, their bodies wrapped together, no inch of skin going un-touched as his hands moved from her back, to her waist, to her ass, to her thighs.

He moaned, his lips still on hers, as she sensed his thrusting increase in speed and intensity. She gripped his shoulders and rode him, the head of his cock reaching further inside of her than she had ever felt a man before. She let the orgasm roll over her like a soft wave, her whole body pulsing and throbbing with pleasure, her lips forming words she couldn't hear.

She leaned her head back, felt her hair hang in the water, and let her orgasm loose, pressing down hard, her entire body clutching him. He moaned, low and loud at the sensation. "Oh God. Sara." He whispered as he came, pulling her close, and held her body tight to his, his lips against her throat.

"Holy shit woman that was," he sighed and leaned his head back.

"I know. I'm amazing. But you're pretty good yourself." She bit his nipple, making him jerk and protest. "But is this gonna be weird now? I mean, I'm not ready for, um," her face flushed with heat at the look in his soft brown eyes.

Craig worked hard to catch his breath. The monster orgasm had caught him by surprise. This woman had been worth the self-imposed wait, but he was alarmed at how his head pounded, how much he ached to have her back, close to him again. He smiled to himself, the natural competitor in him wishing he could send a mental picture to Mr. Gordon right now. He kissed the tip of her nose.

"No. Not weird, at least not to me." He released her and she swam away. He enjoyed the view of her naked body moving through the water. He climbed out, suddenly unsure what to do next.

He wanted her. All of her. But she'd said she was not ready for much beyond…what? The occasional fuck?

He sighed, mentally smacking himself upside the head for letting her get to him, then reached down to ease her up out of the water, wrapping her in a huge towel and resisting the urgent need to kiss her again. Guiding her over to the cushioned lounge chairs on either side of the table where the wine bottle waited, he kept up his mantra: *Just friends. Just friends. Just friends.* But he couldn't resist taking a deep breath of her, his nose buried in her hair as they sat together and sipped the wine.

"So are you going to drive me home or are we camping out poolside tonight," she asked.

"Why not stay, or do you have early appointments tomorrow," he asked, surprising himself. He hadn't really planned it this way. Figured he'd take her home after his carefully choreographed pool seduction. But the urge to wake up with her in his arms was overwhelming to the point of breathtaking.

"Why, do you cook breakfast?" She ran her free hand down his torso, making his skin pebble.

"For your information I am the best blueberry pancake maker on the planet; it's a known fact," he shifted in his seat as her hand traced a path towards his towel already stirring in anticipation.

She took another sip of wine.

"You know, I love blueberry pancakes, so if that's part of the deal, I think I'll stay over. But, you'll have to get me home by eight tomorrow," she said softly as she leaned over to kiss the skin of his chest, and nose her way over to his nipple, which hardened appreciably. He closed his eyes and leaned back on the lounge chair, as she licked her way downward, towards the bulge under his towel.

Contentment slipped over her like the soft towel he wrapped her in, as she snuggled in deeper. When tears sprung up, she cursed herself and sat forward.

"Hey, hey, none of that," he swung his legs down to the floor and gripped her shoulders. "I do not make ladies cry. I won't allow it. Seriously. Cut it out."

She giggled and leaned into his arm. Draping a hand over his muscular thigh, she took a deep breath. "Craig," He tilted her chin up, forcing her to look at him.

"No."

"What? You don't even know what I'm about to ask."

"Whatever it is the answer is no."

"Huh. Well, I guess I can't suck your cock then. Oh well, your loss." She stood, and stretched, yelping when he tugged her back to his lap and covered her lips with his. The kiss left her completely breathless in more ways than one. "So now that we have that covered…" she touched her forehead to his. "This is fun. I'm glad we did it. But you have to know,"

"I know. It's okay. I don't mind being a fuck buddy, Sara. Honestly, I have always had a blast with you anyway; this just adds a lovely, um, element to our friendship, don't you think?"

She smiled and kissed him once more then stood up to reposition herself across his lap, the lovely hard bulge of his resurgent erection warm against her body. "Yes, a lovely element indeed. You got any more of those up here?" She nodded towards the wad of paper towel where he'd placed his used condom.

"Paper towels? Sure, for you anything." He picked her up, locking onto her lips with his and carried her towards the elevator.

"Smart ass," she insisted but held on for dear life, suddenly wanting nothing more than the calm, handsome, charming man holding her in his arms.

He set her down and pressed her against the wall of the elevator, his hand reaching under the towel to caress her still pulsing sex. "Maybe. But in the meantime, let's fuck again, eh buddy?"

"Promises, promises," she sighed as he fulfilled it, once in the elevator and once more on the bed before they fell into an exhausted, sweaty, contended sleep.

CHAPTER NINE

Sara glanced at the text. Her scalp tingled for a split second thinking it was Jack but she smiled when she realized the number was Craig's.

"Hey yourself" she sent back. *"Thanks for Friday night; btw. I can't remember if I said that."*

"Yeah, you did. About a hundred times already. What about Saturday morning? I don't get thanked for that?"

Her face flushed at the memory. *"I think I get the thanks for that."*

"Oh, yeah you do. Thanks."

About an hour went by while she sorted through paperwork for a few closings. His next message tested her resolve to go home by herself tonight. She had a strong need to be alone. She needed to process what was happening to her. Jack had managed to make himself scarce, which had become as annoying as his near-constant presence earlier in the week.

Her psyche still smarted from the last whirlwind of emotion that swirled around her relationship with her ex-fiancé, but Craig was certainly helping. She berated, then reminded, herself that they had completely honest conversations about where she was in her head with regard to their relationship. Craig claimed to understand, wanted to give her space and time to get over Jack, but was unable to resist her, according to him. That did a girl's ego good for certain.

"I'm cooking tonight–dinner is at 7. You bring the wine."

She waited a few minutes–a man who knew his way around a kitchen turned her on almost as much as a man with as talented a tongue as he did. She squeezed her thighs together, sighed and made a snap decision.

"Sure. Sounds good. See you then."

Blake chose that moment to call.

"Hey" he said.

"Hey, what's up?"

"Not much. You heard from mom today?"

"Uh, no, why?" she felt a knot forming in her gut at the thought of Blake having to ask her that question.

"Oh, no reason really. I just hadn't talked to her in about a week, which is weird, so I wondered if you had."

Sara thought a moment.

"I actually did talk to her almost exactly a week ago. She was fine. Dad was fine, but bitching about taking his heart pills or some shit. I think it makes him impotent. Ha! The irony," she rolled her eyes. Their father had been a serial cheater for as long as Sara had been aware of such things. It boggled her mind that her mother, such a smart, beautiful doctor, would put up with his nonsense for so long. Anxiety pinged her consciousness, remembering how Blake had reminded her of this, the night she'd broken it off with Jack.

"Ok, well, I'll let you go..." he trailed off. Sara knew he wanted to say something else.

"What's wrong Blake?" She had a ton of stuff to do but didn't want him to think she wouldn't listen.

"What? I'm fine," he insisted. "Except, well, I don't want to bother you with this, I know you have your own issues."

"Jesus H. Christ Blake! Since when have you ever been a burden to me? All I ever do is cry on your damn shoulder about my love life," she put the phone on her shoulder and checked her email–full, as usual.

"Oh hell, it's just a fucking mess," he sighed.

"What is?" she asked, knowing full well what it was, but wanting him to tell her himself.

"Look, I really have to go," he insisted.

She could hear someone calling his name out in the brewery so decided not to press it. He'd let her know when he was ready.

"Ok, but I should let you know about my new man sometime," she smiled into the phone.

"Oh, I already know babe," he laughed and she felt her tension release. It was no good when her brother was unhinged about something. That was her job. "Everybody does! Including you-know-who and he's the only one who isn't really happy for you." He hung up.

She stared at the phone. Why in the hell she couldn't just have a private life, she had no idea. She couldn't deny that she enjoyed being the center of attention. She was fine with that, but she still wasn't completely convinced she knew what she ultimately wanted. The fact that so many people had already made up their minds about what her life "should be" grated on her nerves like never before.

Suddenly gripped with a strange compulsion, she quickly dialed "mom" and tapped her fingers on the desk waiting for her to answer. She'd never been that close to her parents, but all the craziness going on in her love life lately made her feel bereft and she needed to ask her mother a question.

"Hi honey!" Sara smiled, soothed in a way of daughters by mothers, despite disagreements and past clashes.

"Hey mom. Um, you busy?"

"No, I don't have to be down at the clinic for another half an hour." Sara leaned back in her chair. "Retirement" for her mother had meant diving into volunteerism and then founding a clinic to serve poor women's health needs in the scary inner city somewhere, nowhere near her expensive beach side condo. Much to her father's early chagrin, then once he realized the only way he'd see his wife would be to help; he'd jumped in with both feet. Now they both worked nearly as much as they once did, gratis.

"Okay." Sara suddenly had no words for what she needed to know. She bit her lip.

"What is it Sara?" Her mother had been her first example of getting right to the point. "Blake okay? I know he's having some trouble with Rob. And I hear you have a new boyfriend. How exciting!" Her mother did not sound excited. Sara sighed.

"If you hadn't married Daddy..." she began, and then started over. "I know you told me once there was another, different guy. Why...oh hell," She put a hand over her face.

Her mother stayed quiet. Sara felt herself getting aggravated by it. She pulled herself together. "Why did you stay with him mom? I mean, Jesus, he...I caught him, remember?"

"Honey, you can't equate the choices I made with anything you're going through right now. It's not fair to, well, to anyone."

"I know how you all feel about Jack." She let defensiveness creep into her tone and hated it.

"No, you don't. I'll admit that your dad doesn't like him and the reasons for that probably lie in some similarities in their personalities. But women who bitch and moan that their lives are ruined because they married their fathers are just making excuses, I think."

"But...why?"

"I love your father Sara. I always have. We have split up three times, that last time when he acted like such an idiot and you had to see it. We stayed apart nearly a year, remember?"

"Yeah. Hard to forget it, frankly."

"Exactly. Since you were only sixteen, I didn't feel a need to share with you or Blake how we had resolved it. I should have. That's my fault and probably set you both up for failure in relationships." Sara let a tear slip down her cheek at the sound of her mother's deep sigh from so many miles away.

"No, no, it's okay."

"No, it's not. Listen, you have to wrap your head around the fact that people are not perfect. No man is without his flaws. There is something very, very real that happens between two people. Blake has it with Rob. You, well, shit Sara, you want me just to come out and say it I will," Sara shook her head, even though no one could see her.

"No mom, I probably don't want you to but I think you are anyway." Her heart pounded in her chest and she held the phone in a death grip to her ear.

"Jack loves you honey. I know it. You know it. He's not perfect but…you are so unhappy when you aren't together."

"But he's, I mean, I'm ready to kill him half the time when we are together." She knew she sounded lame.

"So? And the other half?"

Sara slumped back in her seat. "This is not what I needed to hear today."

"Then why did you call me? You need a reality check Sara. Blake's been filling your ear with the bad and jeopardizing his own relationship by being over protective. I told him that. Now you need to hear something else for a change. Jack is not your father. You are not me. You two owe it to yourselves to at least talk, like adults, about…"

"No. Mom. I'm not. I can't. I have…"

"I know, I know. Blake thinks this other guy is perfect. Whatever. Please realize something though honey. You should never measure your success by what your friends and family think of you. Remember only you hold that ruler. If you want to be married, or not. A businesswoman, or not. That is your call and no one else's."

"But," Sara let a familiar anger at her mother's natural tendency to take over, to tell her things she didn't want to hear, surge through her.

"No buts. Get back together with Jack, or don't. But do not lay this at your father's feet. That's a cop out. You are too smart and strong for that. I won't allow it."

"Fine." She stood, needing something to do with her nervous energy.

"I gotta go honey. Dad's waiting in the car. He's taken this clinic thing on in such a huge way; it's exhausting. But, it's better than endless rounds of golf, trust me. I was gonna kill him if I had to do any more of that."

"Mom?" Sara's voice broke as she dropped back into her chair.

"Yes?"

"Never mind."

"Sara, please don't do that. I raised you to be straightforward. If you have a question,"

"What the hell do I do now then? If you're so smart about it. Jesus. I love him. I hate him. I can't live without him. I have a goddamned hole in my chest all day, every day. He wants me to trust him. And I can't. Craig is…he's great, but, I can't do it mom. Jack absorbs me, it's terrifying."

"No honey. It's just love. You have to make up your own mind if you are ready for it. Not Blake's mind. Not my mind. Your mind. I'm sorry I wasn't more honest with you guys when your dad and I finally resolved our shit. That probably would have helped. Let's just say, relationships worth having, take work. Gotta go. Call me later. I love you."

"I love you too," Sara whispered into the dead air after her mother ended the call.

A quick glance at her computer brought a flush to her skin when she saw an email from jgordon@stewart.com with "offer" in the subject line. Her body betrayed her at the sight of it as her scalp prickled and she had to bite her lip to restrain a wide, idiotic smile. *An offer from Jack, eh?* Well, that will make things interesting. She clicked to open the email.

Sure enough, it was an offer on one of her oldest listings and a pretty solid one at that. She called her seller and went through the details while she sent Jack an email acknowledgment at the same time. Counter offer in place, she called Jack.

"Hi," he answered, and could hear a commotion in the background that sounded like kids yelling.

"Hey, um, thanks for the offer."

He remained silent.

"So, well, we have a counter, but I think your buyer will like it."

"I'm listening," he stated, over a fresh round of squealing.

"Where the hell are you Jack? A Jonas Brothers concert?" she was irritated by his nonchalance and knew she had no reason to be.

"No, I'm not. So what's the counter," he asked. He wouldn't rise to her bait or tell her where he was.

"Ok, so we are countering ..."

He cut her off.

"How many times do I have to tell you Sara? *You* are not countering. Your *sellers* are countering. You are just representing them," he sighed. "God, you never listen do you?"

She felt herself tensing up. He had said this before–and he was right. She tended to insert herself as a "partner" with her clients, which is not how Stewarts trained them. They were to remain apart, professional, a representing agent and all that. She sighed.

"Sorry," she cleared her throat and started over. "My sellers are countering with three seventy five to your offer of three sixty– and will give possession at closing, no need for a rent back. They agree to all your other terms but I want to know more about this lender–since when do you let anyone borrow money from the internet Jack?"

It was his turn to sigh.

"Yeah, I know but I have actually talked to a person at this outfit and she swears they are golden, so take it or leave it I guess," His voice became muffled then and she realized he'd put the phone down to talk to someone else. She tapped her foot.

"Well?" she asked. "Can you make three seventy-five work? I mean, the place would easily appraise for four hundred and you and I both know it."

"Fuck." She sighed at his frustration. She felt it every day and hearing his voice calmed her in ways she had forgotten.

"What's the status of the building?" She leaned back, wanting to keep his voice in her ear a bit longer.

"All systems stop and go as usual. Plumbing contractor quit after I caught his flunkies stealing a bunch of copper so that was a good day. The electricians work an average of two-point-five hours a day with four breaks for meals and smokes, I know. I've clocked them. It's a nightmare, thanks for asking." She grinned at his tone. God she missed him. Taking a deep breath she pressed onward, not sure why, but needing to say it, her mother's words ringing around in her brain.

"I miss you."

He snorted. "Funny way of showing it." She frowned, as her face heated up in a way only he could provoke.

"How's Heather?" She bit her lip at the frosty silence on the other end. Why did she do this to herself?

"About as good as that blonde kid, I'd say. They're putting up with us."

"Yeah. Somebody has to I guess. Since we can't."

"Yeah." The silence spooled out, strangely comfortable. Sara sighed.

"Well, I'll let you go."

"Wait. Sara. I…" She sat up, swallowed hard and had the bright and brittle realization that if he asked, she'd go to him. No questions asked. Her chest tightened. She needed him, his words, his touch, his presence. Needed him. Period. But there was still that trust thing.

"No, really I should go Jack. I'm sorry. I shouldn't say things like that."

"Like what, baby? Like that you miss me?" She started to protest but he cut her off. "Do not say a word. Just listen a minute, if you can. I miss you too, like a fucking phantom limb do you understand? You are a crucial, functioning part of me, always will be. But I get it. I'm a shit. I won't deny it. But I'll never, ever be happy or complete without you."

She sucked in a breath.

My God. Her natural reaction won out and she winced even as she spoke. "Wow Jack, been watching Oprah or something?"

His bitter laugh brought sudden tears to her eyes. "I'm sorry." She whispered. "Who's the shit now, huh?"

"Yeah. We're quite the pair."

His voice went muffled again but she could hear him speak.

"That's fine babe, I'll see you at home later."

Her brain processed that he must be with Heather somewhere. He had just said "see you at home… Her face flushed hotter and she stood, ready to end the more than scary conversation now.

"Sorry Sara, I just… he trailed off. "Oh hell, never mind."

"Uncle Jack! Uncle Jack!" she heard distinctly.

What the hell? It hit her that she still truly had no concept of his life outside of real estate and women.

"I gotta go. I'll pass on their counter. I think I can make it work. Bye" and he hung up.

She sat for a solid five minutes and stared at her phone, as if it would spill all the answers to her questions. *Uncle Jack?* She reminded herself to ask Rob about Jack's family. Now that the whole town knew she had moved on apparently, perhaps he wouldn't be so pissed if she asked. His words clattered around in her brain like marbles; her skin went hot and cold in turns as she replayed it again and again.

Her mother's outburst of advice, telling her to realize it as love, that relationships meant work. What the hell was that supposed to mean? She knew how to work. She just could not trust this guy. Her mother had no idea what she was talking about; or did she?

She glanced at her watch and saw she only had about two hours to get home, fit in a run, clean up and get over to Craig's.

Craig.

Oh yeah, she had nearly forgotten about him. She took a deep shuddering breath and headed to her car, remorse in her heart, tears in her eyes. Jack was right. She shouldn't involve Craig any further in this. Poor guy. He had done nothing to deserve standing in between two of the most difficult humans on the planet as they played their stupid games, in an apparent attempt to destroy each other. It was a recipe for unhappiness for everyone. She squared her shoulders and wiped her eyes before pulling out into the evening traffic. She'd cut it off with him as soon as she got there.

"Hey, hold on there, sport." Jack swung the small boy up onto his shoulder, letting the girl clamor up his arm as they exited the playground. Their compact, warm bodies felt solid against his skin.

"Uncle Jack! Let's play catch!" The little girl dashed toward the huge bag of crap their mother had lugged to the park with them, producing three gloves and a ball. He grinned, dropped the boy to the ground and spent a blissful half hour tossing the ball around letting them fill the air with their four-year-old chatter. He finally got them piled into the car, keeping the top down as they wanted, even though it threatened rain. After thoroughly ruining all of their dinner with giant scoops of Washtenaw Dairy ice cream cones, he tugged their floppy bodies from the car outside his house. His sister stood in the kitchen, tending to something that smelled delicious on his stove.

"Toss them in the bathtub, throw some shampoo at them and shut the door, quick." She advised. He did, loving the easy way they chattered to him, and made a giant mess of his huge Jacuzzi tub. He shut the door, images of Sara here with him, with their child giggling away in the tub nearly made him pass out with longing.

Fuck. Get a grip.

He leaned on the door a minute, getting his ping-ponging emotions under control. Mo, his sister, nearly seven years his junior, read him like a book and he had no desire to discuss his failed relationship with her. Not after the conversation they'd had today. He bounded down the steps, grabbed a beer from the fridge and leaned against the counter. Maureen bustled around, put out plates of homemade macaroni and cheese, grilled chicken and salad for them. She hollered up the steps.

"Do not drown in there or ruin Uncle Jack's bathroom!" Squeals of laughter echoed down the stairwell. "They're good for another hour at least. Sit. Eat. Talk to me."

He watched as Maureen poured herself a glass of wine and sank into the chair opposite him. They'd come back for a few weeks to visit family, mostly Brandis'. All she had left of family now was Jack. He loved her and had been a solid big brother to her from the beginning, as their parents were more or less out of the picture by the time she'd had come along. Their mother, a functional alcoholic and their father...well, another story altogether. Jack grinned at his sister.

"Missed you." He raised his glass.

"I thought I'd be attending a wedding on this trip. What the fuck, Jack?" Cutting right to the chase, as usual.

He grimaced, took a bite of the amazing, rich, cheesy concoction she'd conjured out of his pantry, stalling. She glared at him, tapping her long finger on the table. Mo stood a stunning, thin five-foot nine-inches, and boasted an athletic body and as hot a temper to rival her brother's. "Stop stalling and answer me. What did you do?"

"Look, Mo, I don't want to talk about it."

"Tough shit. Could you salvage it?"

He sighed and put his chin in his hand, reliving their talk today. Dear God he missed her. Wished every single fucking day for that one moment back, where he didn't say, "You're right" and he could change things and say, "You're wrong. Those condoms are from another life. The one I lived before I found you. I love you please don't leave."

"Sweetie," his sister gave him a sympathetic look. "I'm sorry."

"Yeah, my fault. End of story."

"But, maybe if..."

He held up a hand. "No. Discussion over." She glared at him then to his surprise, stood, and brought a chair close to him, sitting so their knees touched, holding both of his hands.

"Cut the shit John Patrick. You are miserable. I've never seen you like this." He tried to pull his hand out of her grip. "Get her back. I don't care what you did. Surely you can fix it?"

"Not likely." He looked away. She grabbed his chin, turned him to face her. Their matching blue eyes clashed. She smiled.

"I don't believe that for a minute. Try. You need her. I don't even know her and I want her for you."

"All right enough, ya bossy bitch. Go eat your food. Those spawns of yours need to eat too."

She stood, put a hand on his shoulder. "Don't screw this one up this time brother. I think it's the real deal. And that Heather?" She made a dismissive sound. "Don't like her. Get rid of her."

"Yes'm," he grinned into his wine glass. "I'll get right on that for you."

"Oh fuck you, you pompous asshole."

"So dainty. Do you kiss my friend with that mouth?"

"Yep, among other things." She put her chin on her hands and batted her eyes at him. He groaned.

"Ick. Spare me." They both jumped up at the sound of a crash and a loud cry. Jack took the steps two at a time, grabbed his niece from the slippery floor, holding her close, wrapping her in a towel and soothing her, loving the opportunity to be loved, unconditionally, for the sheer comfort he could provide. The sounds of Mo berating the girl's brother for shoving her out of the tub made him smile.

And miss Sara even more.

CHAPTER TEN

Sara leaned out onto the balcony rail and admired the view of Ann Arbor from Craig's condo. She smelled the steaks on the grill, heard him moving around inside, prepping everything else. She squirmed, uneasy, mad at herself. She intended to put a stop to this before it went any further, before she entangled him any deeper in her stupid melodrama.

She smiled at him as he approached with the wine bottle. Her friend. Her amazingly hot, blonde, tan, gorgeous, romantic, friend with an absolute proven ability to please. She was wet already watching him. Her heart fluttered.

As if reading her thoughts, he grabbed her hand and pulled her inside. Once they hit the kitchen, he spun her around so she was leaning against the huge granite island. He kissed her deeply, making her sigh with pleasure as she wound her arms around his neck, burying her hands in his hair.

Craig broke their contact and grabbed her around the waist to lift her onto the island. She smiled to herself as he unzipped her jeans and pulled them and her panties down and tossed them aside.

"Um, Craig, I think something is burning," she tapped him on the shoulder as he pulled her knees apart, headed towards her bare pussy.

"What," he muttered. "Oh, shit."

He left her to pull the potatoes out of the oven before they ruined. He flipped the oven off and walked the few steps back to where she sat perched on the island, naked from the waist down.

Stop, remember Sara? Don't take this any further. It's not fair, especially to him.

He smiled at her and leaned on the counter, running a finger from her lips, down her neck, to her t-shirt until he reached the bottom of it and lifted it up and over her head.

Oh, well, maybe after just one more time.

She giggled, mentally scolding herself, and raised her arms up so he could take it off, exposing her bare breasts and rock hard nipples.

"Nice," he said as he leaned in to take one in his mouth.

"Mmmmm, no, that's nice," she muttered as she wound her hands in his hair again. She pulled him around the corner of the island so he was once again between her legs and wrapped both legs around him to hold him close. He ran his hands through her hair and down her neck to her shoulders.

"God, you are just gorgeous, you know that," he said as he switched from one nipple to another. Her skin kept heating up, her clit throbbed by the time he let his lips and tongue draw a wet line from her breasts, down her stomach to her navel. She gasped at the sensation as he dipped his tongue in there, and then continued downwards as her hips began to move to give him better access.

He stood up suddenly and reached behind her to move the tray of bread aside.

"Lie back Sara, right here," he told her before he kissed her again, leaving her breathless. "I want you to come, right now," he stated as he pulled her hips towards his mouth.

She leaned back on her elbows and bent one knee up placing her foot on the chilly granite counter. She stared at him as he lunged up between her legs, moving towards her lips once more to caress her with his mouth and tongue.

Breaking their contact, he fluttered over her nipples and the pebbled skin of her stomach before finally settling himself between her legs.

"Oh, God," Sara cried out as her pussy contracted. "Wow, ahhh, Craig, don't stop." She propped both feet on his back as her body relaxed and her hips started thrusting against his mouth.

He broke his exquisite contact with her clit and licked his way downward, dipping his tongue in and out of her pussy. He made a satisfied sound deep in his throat, took a moment to lick and nibble the insides of each thigh. Sara was too close to orgasm to allow for a break from his lips and she put her hands on his head to guide him back to her center.

"Don't stop," she reminded him as she lay back fully onto the counter, her legs still around his shoulders.

He reached down to adjust his erection and complied. She raised her hips so he didn't have to crouch to reach her and gave in to the orgasm at it rolled over her, coating his lips with her passion. She shuddered, and Craig stood back up.

"Hey, you said you wanted me to come," she said, her eyes still closed, the granite starting to chill her back.

Craig watched her willing his erection down. He wanted this to be a slow night of pleasure and that meant waiting on his part. His plan to drive "friends," "benefits," and most especially "Jack Gordon" out of her mind and life forever had shifted into overdrive.

"So let's eat," he stated and started to grab her hand to pull her up.

"Wait, wait, let me just lie here a minute," she muttered and leaned back on her elbows to watch him. "You know what, I think it's your turn lover boy," she said, her eyes hooded. She smiled at him and licked her lips. "Take it out."

Craig raised an eyebrow at her. She looked devastating, lying there on the kitchen island, completely naked, one leg still bent at the knee, the other swinging in anticipation. His cock stiffened to the point of near pain. He sighed and realized that he would not be the one in control tonight, or very possibly, ever.

He released his aching shaft from its denim bondage. Keeping their distance, he started to rub himself from base to tip eyes fixed on hers.

"Nice," she muttered. "Keep going. Like you mean it."

His hand took on a familiar rhythm, and he took a step back to lean against the wall to brace himself. He'd give her a show if she wanted, but he got to watch too.

"Touch yourself, Sara," he said from across the room. "Show me."

Her finger started to trace her still sensitive clit and down to her wet lips. She climbed down and started towards him.

"No," he held a hand up and stood up straighter. "Stay there. Show me more." She wasn't the only one who got to make the rules, he thought as he brought his hand back to his own cock.

She shrugged and leaned back again, still propped on one elbow, her other hand starting to rub at her clit more urgently, as she watched him resume his own hand job.

Craig settled back against the wall again, and watched her—watched her incredible pussy pulse and throb as he rubbed his own fluid up and down his length. He imagined her enveloping him, felt that pussy he was watching across the room taking him in, holding him tight in its velvet vise and he increased his hand speed. He sensed the comfortable, familiar surge of energy and blood as his orgasm approached.

He groaned when she leaned up and plunged her fingers into herself, felt a familiar tingling at the base of his spine, the release quick, urgent and satisfying.

He closed his eyes, took a deep breath, then opened them and stared at her, his hand still wrapped around himself. She smiled and jumped down from the island, covered the distance between them in two steps and pressed her lips over his.

"Mmm," he muttered when she ended their kiss before he said something stupid, something that gave away how much his chest constricted when he held her close. "Fun. But now I'm really hungry," he grinned at her, pushed his hair up off his forehead and tucked his cock back inside his jeans. "Need a new shirt though," he laughed and pulled the cum-stained one off, heading into the bedroom.

He hesitated for a minute, and stared in the mirror on the wall of his bedroom, reminding himself to take it easy, not to get too attached to her. He knew she had a long way to go before Gordon was out of her system and that her brave words about "just needing a friend" might be true now, but he had plans to change that, ones that required patience on his part. He squared his shoulders and walked back out into the living room and into the kitchen. She leaned against the island where she'd just recently climaxed all over his face, sipping her wine. His skin prickled and he had to bite his tongue to keep from picking her up her up and carrying her into the bedroom.

"Yo. You letting the steaks burn or what?" He hollered, grabbing a beer and fixing a smile on his face.

"Raw food takes one look at me and burns, and I do not mean that as a compliment. I am a rotten cook, hate the thought of it, and rely heavily on the men in my life to keep me from starving to death." She tossed over her shoulder before going out on the patio to poke at the slabs of beef he'd laid on the grill, wine glass still in hand. By the time he reached her, tears streamed down her face.

"Whoa, whoa there, sweets. You forget my rule already? Craig does not make girls cry." He put an arm around her shoulder, and acknowledged that this whole thing might be harder than he thought.

Sara lay awake, listening to the night sounds of Craig's condo, including the deep inhale and exhale of the man next to her. She put a hand over her eyes.

You are such a shit. You said you wouldn't do this to him. God!

She sat, holding the soft blanket to her breasts, breathing shallow.

No need to panic. Wake him up and tell him. Tell him you are leaving and never coming back. Do it now Sara, before it's too late.

A hand grabbed her shoulder and pulled her back down into the warm nest of bedding. She smelled his cologne, the pool, their combined passion when he pulled her close from behind. "Lie down. I've got you." She closed her eyes, allowed herself a minute of calm before easing out from under his arm. He propped himself on an elbow and blinked in the light of the bedside lamp. "What time is it?" He rolled onto his back, his near perfect, slim, naked form exposed, his cock stirring to attention again. She bit her lip.

"It's around four I think. I gotta go." She yanked her jeans on, shoved her arms into her tee shirt, fury rising at her own stupid behavior. He simply watched her, arms behind his head. Finally, after a few minutes of silence she stuck her feet into sandals and stared at him.

Speak Sara. You owe it to him.

"Look, Craig, I'm not..." She held up a hand as he started to get out of bed. "No, don't."

"Gotta take a leak, sorry. I'm listening." She rolled her eyes and sunk into a large leather chair. He emerged from the bathroom, drying his hands, dressed in a pair of soft shorts. He sat at the end of the bed, elbows on knees and gazed at her.

She took a deep breath. "I'm not who you need me to be right now."

He raised an eyebrow. "It was my understanding that you were my friend. Are you not that anymore?" She sighed and rubbed her eyes.

"No. I mean, yes. I am your friend, but, this," she made a circling motion with her finger. "All this between us now has to stop."

"Why? You don't like it?" He leaned back on the bed, propped a foot on the bed. She frowned at him.

"Don't ask me rhetorical questions. You know I like it. That's not the issue." She stood. "I'm gonna head home."

He stood, put a hand on her arm, his touch firm and confident. "Don't go." She stared down at his arm then into his eyes before pulling out of his grip. She had a hand on the cold chrome door handle when he spoke, making her heart leap into her throat. "You are seriously going to let him keep you from finding happiness aren't you?"

She clenched her jaw, turned slowly and leaned back against door, staring at him. He stood across the dimly lit room. Odors of grilled meat, exhaust from the street below, and the ever-present chlorine filled her senses. "What the hell is that supposed to mean? You think you have me figured out, do you? Got all the answers I need?"

He shrugged, crossed his arms over his bare chest. "No, I never said that. Don't put words in my mouth."

She sighed and looked up at the ceiling. The need to escape overwhelmed her. She couldn't face this right now. Her head pounded from all the turmoil.

"Go on. I'll catch you later." He threw up his hands and started back into the bedroom.

"No, Craig, wait. I'm sorry. You don't deserve all my bullshit. That's why I'm leaving. Can't you get that?" He stopped, put both hands on the doorjamb and hung his head.

"Fine, Sara. Then go. Spare me all your bullshit. Thanks in advance." Without looking back, he went into the bedroom and shut the door.

CHAPTER ELEVEN

"So, where is he, this Prince Charming," Rob asked. "Blake is walking around making wedding plans and shit, so I guess I need to meet him."

Sara shot Blake a glance. He shrugged. She stifled her impulse to smack him and confront him with his own relationship problems. She didn't want to cause a scene but he'd be hearing from her about it very soon. Besides, she had her own issues, as usual.

"He's not coming. And he's just a friend anyway so cool your matrimonial jets."

"Really? I thought that was him over there." Blake jerked his chin towards the door. It didn't escape her notice that he and Rob stayed on opposite sides of the bar, and wouldn't meet each other eyes.

She felt Craig's hands on her shoulders before she had a chance to turn and see him. She tensed a moment, then relaxed and smiled at him. He leaned in to brush her lips with his.

"Hi guys. I'm Craig, Sara's friend." He stuck out his hand.

"That's right Rob. We are friends. So keep commentary to a minimum please."

Sara leaned her chin on her hand a moment and watched him. Her surprise faded to relief that he had showed up. She didn't have it in her to explain the odd turn things had taken lately. She and Jack had reverted to the sort of nightly check-in calls about their deal, just as they had done the year before. The difference this time marked a sea of change in their relationship. It seemed as long as they remained physically separate, they communicated beautifully.

She'd stayed up into the wee hours, snuggled down under her covers, chatting with him about anything and everything. Her brother and Rob, her parents and the strange, stilted relationship she maintained with them. He filled her in about his sister, Maureen, who'd married one of his best friends from high school and moved to Germany for her husband's army career. When he spoke of his niece and nephew, the man sounded positively moony—or as moony as a guy like Jack could sound. No topic was off limits, except of course their own failed relationship.

"Going back to the club," he'd told her last night making her scalp tingle.

"Oh? With..."

"Yeah. She says she wants to try it out. I am fairly confident she won't care for it, but whatever. I'm willing to give it a shot. You know me, anything to make you ladies happy."

She closed her eyes, shutting out the banter between her brother and her …. Lover? Friend?

Jesus, what a mess.

The thought of Jack with that woman, in her submissive position made Sara want to scream and throw things. But, she'd had him and she'd given him back, hadn't she?

Yes, she had.

"Well, have fun."

He'd stayed silent a moment, letting it gather power between them.

"I would, if you were with me."

"Jack. Stop it. Talk about something else. We were doing so well."

"Sorry. I don't know about you but I need some sleep. Tomorrow night will be a late one for me." She had to bite her lip not to cry out with jealousy at that.

"Suppose so. I have a date too." Of course, at that time, she'd figured Craig wouldn't show. Not after the disappearing act she'd pulled.

"Nice. Tell surfer boy hello for me."

She'd yawned, stretched and run her hand over her breasts, wishing beyond reason for his touch. "Maybe. 'Night Jack. Sleep well."

"I would, if you were with me."

She laughed. "Stop it. 'Night."She ended the call, a lightness in her soul at his last words.

"Sara," Blake snapped his fingers at her. "Hey, where did you go? C'mon, let's hit it or we'll be late," he pulled her to her feet and turned her over to Craig who put a hand on her back to guide her out the door.

He still hadn't spoken a single word to her.

No matter how hard he fought it, Craig knew he'd fallen for her, precaution and self-preservation be damned.

He watched her one day in the office as she went about her business and suddenly began fantasizing about how he'd ask her to marry him–how he'd solicit her brother's help planning the most perfect evening because he knew Blake liked him and he'd figured out that was key. The small voice of doubt that would raise its hand to be heard at times, especially those times when Craig found himself flat out gloating over Jack Gordon's loss, he forced down beneath his desire for her.

When she had glanced over at him and smiled, breaking his reverie, he'd had to shake himself to banish the image of Jack watching them. Of him pounding into her while that asshole had to observe them, powerless to change how she felt.

After that night, when she'd left without warning or a decent explanation he'd nearly given up. Something held her back, kept her at arm's length. Maybe it was the friend thing. Maybe he had read too much into it too soon. He sighed as they exited The Ark, Ann Arbor's funky, indie music venue after the concert.

"Let's get a beer. I want to go over the Big House Brewing. I haven't been and I heard…" She squeezed his hand suddenly and gave him a significant look. "What?"

"It's okay babe." Blake gave her a one armed hug, shot his boyfriend a murderous look and walked away, leaving Rob to shrug and follow him.

"Sorry. What did I say?"

"Suzanne Baxter, one of the owners there, she was, um, Blake's last girlfriend I guess you could say. It's awkward and something is going on between those two lately." She shrugged and took his hand. "I'm glad you came tonight."

He smiled and put an arm around her shoulder. "You are a high maintenance bitch. But I wouldn't have missed this concert for anything."

She punched his side, and then wound an arm around his waist, reveling in his familiar scent. "Let's get that beer. I'll buy."

"Damn straight you will, walking out on me, leaving me in my cold lonely bed. Jeez. I felt like a de-flowered abandoned prom date."

She laughed. "C'mon, I can drive."

By the time they reached the Tap Room of Big House Brewing Co, it was nearly full but they found a seat at the crowded bar and ordered a couple of the dark stout beers that had made the company regionally famous. The silence between them felt awkward but he let it linger. As he glanced around, his gaze lit on a slight, redheaded woman making her way through the crowd, laughing and chatting.

"That's Suzanne," Sara whispered. Craig kept watching as she worked the room. "She dumped Blake, telling him he was too young. It broke his heart I tell you. Within a month, he'd met Rob and fell even harder so maybe it was meant to be, who could know? Fate. It's a bitch." She finished her pint and raised her hand for another.

He couldn't tear his eyes away from the woman for some reason. At one point, she looked up and met his gaze, making him blush and turn around.

A few minutes later, the woman was beside them with a hand on Sara's shoulder and a genuine smile on her lovely face. "Sara? How are you?"

Sara returned her grin, stood and hugged her. "I'm okay Suze, thanks. This is Craig Robinson, a friend and fellow realtor at Stewarts." He shook her hand.

"Great to meet you. Hey, um Sara, can I talk to you a sec?"

"Not if it's about Jack you can't." Craig stared at the red headed beauty. *How in the hell did she know...*

"Sorry, Craig." His skin buzzed when Suzanne put a hand on his arm. "Small town. Too many connections. Anyway," She gave Sara a look. "We'll talk later, okay?"

He watched a frown crease Sara's face as she repeated: "Not if it's about Jack. That subject is closed."

Suzanne laughed and held up a hand. "All right sorry. Just trying to …"

"Don't." Sara stared straight ahead. Craig smiled at Suzanne and shrugged.

"Caught in the middle, that's me." She put an arm around his shoulders, startling him but he went with it.

"Don't know if that's a safe place between those two, dear." She gave him a squeeze and backed away. The look in her eyes was inscrutable. He had a sudden urge to keep her around, chatting. She patted his arm, winked and moved back into the crowd. He stared after her a minute, seemingly mesmerized.

Damn. That was strange.

He turned and focused back on Sara. But the deep blue gaze of the lovely redheaded Suzanne stayed in his head.

CHAPTER TWELVE

Blake stared out of the car window, tapping his fingers on his knee as Rob maneuvered through the crowded Ann Arbor streets. He put a hand on his lover's thigh at one point, as they neared his small house on the west side. Rob parked, stared at the windshield, then up at him in a way that turned his blood cold.

"I can't do this anymore Blake." He kept a death grip on the steering wheel.

"Do what anymore?" Blake put his palm over Rob's white knuckles but the other man didn't move. "Rob?"

"You are not over her. I get it. Sara is miserable still. My friend Jack, whom you despise, is equally unhappy. This is a mess. I need some space."

"Okay." Blake kept staring at him, willing him to look back. He finally did and Blake started at the unshed tears glistening in the man's eyes. "Really?"

He turned back to face forward, let go of the wheel and climbed out of the car without another word. Blake got out, practically ran around the front of the thing to get to him, terror gripping his heart. Clutching Rob's biceps he pressed him back against the SUV's side. "Really?" he repeated, his jaw clenched. Rob stared at him a minute. Blake started to say something,

anything, to beg the man not to go. To take back what he said about
needing space. But his lover's mouth cut him off. Rob thrust his
tongue between Blake's lips, held him close. The kiss tasted hard,
desperate, and Blake nearly came apart at the seams as Rob
threaded his hands through his hair and tugged at it.

They broke apart, breathing hard. Blake smiled at him but
Rob's next words froze him in place. "I'm moving out. Just for a
while." He put a hand against Blake's jaw. "I love you, you stupid,
stubborn man. But you have to get your head straight."

"Rob, Jesus, we've been through this. I am over her. I…I'm
leaving Sara alone. Just like you asked me to."

"I am done sharing my bed with the Suzanne." Blake
gasped when Rob grabbed the back of his neck, pulled him close
again, so close he could smell the kitchen on him. So close, he
could taste him again. He took a breath. "Oh hell," Rob groaned and
slanted his mouth over Blake's smothering him with need, want, and
something unnamed. Something Blake obviously could not provide.

Blake caressed the back of his lover's neck, and then broke
the kiss. Leaning his forehead against Rob's, he shifted, making
room for his stiffening cock. "I love you Rob Freitag. I'm sorry I've
been such a shit lately. Don't leave me. Not even for a minute.
Okay?" His heart pounded in his ears and he increased his grip on
Rob's neck, tugging at the man's hair.

"Open your eyes." Rob's voice was low, ominous. Blake
did, not realizing he'd even closed them. "We rushed into this. I…
we have a lot in common and have made a huge success of the
business, but you are going in a direction that I don't want. I know
you. I know you still obsess over her. And I told you I am fucking
finished sharing you with her." He tore himself out of Blake's
embrace and stomped towards the front steps, leaving Blake
gripping air, then the car window in an effort not to scream in
frustration.

When he reached the front door, the tall, blonde man turned
to face Blake who remained hanging on for dear life. He could not
lose Rob. He had to fix this. Now. "Come on inside. Let's talk more.
I'm sorry. It was a shit day. I'm tired and I need a drink."

Blake took a breath and pushed himself up off the car, willing to take responsibility for his part of this. "You're right." He barely heard his own voice. The last months of his Sara's drama with Gordon and Suzanne's coincidental insertion back into his life as a result had thrown him. Thoughts of her had returned, with a vengeance.

Rob walked back to the top of the porch steps. "I know I am baby. Now come on in, let's talk a little more."

Blake trudged up the steps, heart heavy; the bitter taste of defeat in his mouth once again.

Jack gritted his teeth and drove into the night, making his way into the interior of Detroit, to a tall, nondescript building that housed one of the most exclusive BDSM clubs in the entire Midwest. The woman sitting next to him would not shut up. She'd been babbling like an idiot since they'd left the house. He'd come home, exhausted, wanting nothing more than a shower and a nap, preferably one with his ex-fiancée, and found Heather, in full French maid costume, a four-course meal spread out on the dining room table.

He'd made the best of it. He did love great food, and recalled thinking he'd have to hire a cook after he and Sara got married as neither of them darkened the kitchen door beyond making coffee. But they weren't getting married and he'd let this tall, angular, acerbic woman re-attach herself to him like a barnacle.

Why?

Because he couldn't be alone? Needed some sort of female justification for his existence? Couldn't go more than a few days without getting laid?

He ran a hand down his face. He'd made her wait. Not allowed her to touch him or vice versa, trying to explain they'd get enough of each other at the club, and that she'd be expected to act a certain way once there. She wouldn't listen.

Christ this was a huge mistake.

Evan and Julie kept up the conversational end from the back seat, letting the woman babble. He glanced at her. She certainly looked the part, in a leather bustier, garters, and long black leather coat plus knee-high boots. Her coal black curtain of hair shone and her deep brown eyes sparkled when they caught his. He smiled, tried to muster a semblance of desire for what lay ahead.

He failed.

He had on a dark suit, expensive tie and felt the part anyway. The whole thing reeked of desperation. He had finally figured something else out. He clutched Heather's leg.

"Have you been drinking?"

"Uh, maybe a little but…"

"I told you not to. Alcohol brings too much potential for danger at these places–the real ones anyway."

"I didn't bring a flask for God's sake." She crossed her arms and pouted. He looked in the rearview mirror and caught his friend's eye. He and Evan had been popular at this particular club many years ago, before Jack had given up the lifestyle and headed into a long series of affairs, fucking and dumping more women than he cared to remember, trying to get the bitter taste of failure out of his system. "Natural Masters," they'd been called and had been in high demand on weekends. He did get off on the scene; that much had remained. After a while, it all felt empty, sad, and pitiful when he had to leave for home alone, yet again. Not a single submissive he played with ever compelled him enough to go beyond that.

Evan and Julie were now married, but still liked to participate, getting off on the exhibitionism of places like The Suite. He sighed. This whole thing felt wrong, but he'd told her he'd bring her, the woman who now occupied his life, but nothing more. Unable to stop thinking of the way he and Sara chatted every night, how he needed that simple conversational connection more than anything, he glanced at his watch. Nearly eleven. When they usually started talking, or at least had for the last week or so. He would've given his left nut to be doing that, listening to the slightly breathy sound of her laugh, to her tiny lisp, instead of going anywhere near this scene with the woman seated next to him.

Before he knew it they'd arrived, he'd handed keys to the valet and gone up to the top floor. Heather clutched his arm, practically jumping up and down in anticipation. Evan shot him a sympathetic look. He shrugged, put a hand in his pocket and tried to conjure images of the woman he wanted here, on her knees, with him. When the elevator doors slid open, revealing a deep red and black, once familiar, lobby his throat closed up in panic. He let his friend lead him out, back into the dark heart of a world he thought he'd left behind forever. Taking a deep breath, he smiled and greeted the owner, letting the sights, sounds, and smells permeate his psyche and bring out the part of his personality that he had kept under wraps, let loose for a while with Sara, and then wrestled back into place once again.

CHAPTER THIRTEEN

Sara made her way through the throng at the Michigan / Michigan State football game tailgate party. Arbor Title always threw the biggest, most elaborate of these tented parties on the golf course opposite the Big House–Michigan Stadium, which seated over a hundred thousand people. The day boasted picture perfect football weather: sunny, about sixty-five degrees, and she stood, sipping an early beer and watching the crowd.

Craig had clients that morning, hoped to show up about an hour before kickoff. She'd never felt more alone in a giant crowd of people, many of whom she considered friends. A heaviness settled over her. An unhappiness she knew could be remedied by one man, if she'd just allow it. But she couldn't. Greg Stewart pulled her into a conversation with a few lenders, but her mind wandered. When he handed her a ticket to the game, she tucked it into her back pocket, thinking she'd likely skip it but thanked him anyway and moved away from the group.

Blake and Rob stood on the other side of the tent, talking with some city council members. Blake looked like he'd lost weight and she did not like the dark circles under his eyes. At one point, he caught her gaze and lifted his glass to her. She smiled, blew a kiss. She'd been avoiding him for at least a week, she knew it. The pallor of his skin was alarming. She started towards him, determined to clear the air between them.

The sound of Jack's unmistakable laughter pierced her foggy brain. She turned, and the vision of him in full Michigan State regalia with the lovely Heather attached to him like a parasite greeted her, making her stomach lurch into her throat.

Mine.

No. Not anymore. She closed her eyes.

"Sara!" The sound of her friend Val's voice broke through the haze of worry about her brother and fury at the sight of Jack with that woman. "Where's Craig?"

"Oh, um, he's coming later. Had clients." Her eyes kept wandering back to him, tall, handsome, dressed in green, but so was half of the crowd. Ann Arbor was lousy with State alums. She herself boasted a degree from the hometown university and wore her block M proudly. Val put an arm around her.

"You look terrible. What's wrong?"

"Oh, nothing. Sorry. Worried about Blake, overworked, you know."

She moved away, unwilling to discuss how much her late night conversations with Jack kept her going. Last night he'd told her about the disastrous venture to the BDSM club. She couldn't help but glare at the silly woman at his side.

"Then why in the hell won't you cut her lose Jack? If you're that miserable? I mean unless there are redeeming qualities...." She'd let her voice fade. Let him read between her lines.

He'd laughed; a slightly ugly sound that made her wince. "Yeah, I'm calling it off. But I already promised her we'd go to this game."

"You're stalling. For a guy who gets off on negotiation, who has dumped enough women to fill Michigan Stadium, you are sure being a pussy about Heather."

"Lovely. Thanks for the moral support."

"Sorry. Blunt. That's me."

"Yeah. I know. Anyway, I had to put her in a taxi and send her home from the club. It was a mess. Ever since she's been trying to force me to "punish" her, to control me with some kind of fucked up reverse domination thing. Christ."

"Topping from the bottom?"

"Well, somebody's been doing more research."

She'd grinned into the phone, pressed a hand to her mound. God she wanted him. So much. Needed him like she needed to drink water to survive.

"Are you touching yourself Sara?" His growly voice got lower, making her nipples harden in instant response.

"I'm not having phone sex with you Jack."

"I just asked a simple question."

She sighed; let one finger linger over her clit, suppressing a groan at the sensation.

"Are you? Tell me baby. I'll gladly walk you through it."

The compulsion to do that, to let him bring her to orgasm with his voice nearly made her cry. She yanked her hand away, sat up, and wiped her eyes. "No. I'm not. I'm gonna go now. Guess I'll see you tomorrow. At the tailgate."

"Yeah. Guess so. I sure would love to hear that sound you make again. The little one, right before you…"

"Stop it. G'night."

She mentally snapped back to the present, smiled at whoever stood in front of her, and made her way as far from Jack and his tall, exotic date as she could. Part of her thought he might be bullshitting about Heather, telling her one thing while living another. At one point, scalp tingling with recognition as she chatted with a few title company folks, she looked around, and caught his deep blue gaze fixed right on her. His half smile, wry, a little sad, made her clench her fists.

Mine.

No, not anymore. You let go of him for perfectly legitimate reasons.

Craig made his way into the tent, already teeming with hundreds of mostly drunk tailgaters, in various forms of blue and yellow or green and white. The ice luge was in full use, and he chuckled at the people accepting freezing cold shots of whatever liquor at the bottom of the huge thing. He grabbed a beer and a plate, starving and anxious to see Sara.

He spotted her, finally, but ended up sidetracked by a few lenders he'd been working with, shot the shit a while, ate a burger and downed a beer and a half before looking around again. Arbor Title knew how to throw a party. The booze and food abounded, a DJ cranked it out, five huge televisions tuned to pre-game festivities.

"Craig," the sound of his name made him turn. He grinned.

"Suzanne," the woman gave him a huge hug. He let her, his usual reticence about public displays of affection out the window. "Great to see you again." He looked up to see two giant banners over the bar, one with "Big House Brewing," the other "The Local."

"Dueling breweries, eh?" She glanced back.

"Oh, yeah, kinda. You're empty," she pointed to his bottle. "Let me grab you one." He followed her, losing sight of Sara in the process as the crowd gained momentum and volume. Once reinforced, he sipped, leaning on the portable bar next to Suzanne.

"What got you into the beer business anyway? You a brewer?"

She laughed and leaned into him. Her proximity made his skin tighten, but he knew she did it so he could hear her over the ever-increasing din. "My late husband left me a huge wad of cash. I've known Evan since elementary school. I needed something to take my mind off the fact I had a late husband and I know how to sell stuff. The rest is history." She took a sip, keeping her bright blue eyes on his.

"Sorry. About the late husband, I mean. I didn't know."

"Yeah, it sucked being a widow at thirty. He was forty-five, and had done well for us. We had no kids, and after about three years of intense mourning, I brought my money to the Big House Brewing Co. and haven't looked back."

Craig smiled and put a hand on her shoulder, then removed it when he caught sight of Sara at the other bar, seemingly arguing with her brother. "Excuse me a minute," his chest tightened at the sight of her as it always did.

Images of her Sara's body over his the night they made love, and the night after the concert crowded his newly addled brain. He knew then she'd been a million miles away. He'd still held onto her all night long, even later when he'd felt tears drip onto his arm, when she thought he was asleep.

What a mess.

He wiped his face, let physical and emotional exhaustion steal over him. Following the trajectory of Blake's pointing finger over to the far side of the tent. In between all the laughing drunkenness, he got a clear view of Jack. The man had a tall, exotic-looking brunette he knew as the infamous "Heather" attached to one arm, but stared across the sea of people at Sara.

Craig clenched his fists and moved closer, ignoring the warning hand Suzanne put on his arm.

"You are out of control, you know that? Jesus, Blake, I'm allowed to be in the same room with the guy. We fucking *work* together!" Suzanne tightened her grip, stopping him in his tracks.

"Wait. She needs to say this." Suzanne stood beside him, close enough that he could smell the subtle floral of her perfume. "He *is* out of control. Blake has got to let go of the big brother over-protectiveness or he's gonna make everyone crazy. Poor guy." She sighed and leaned into him, making him startle but gave him the chance to do exactly what he wanted, to put what he hoped seemed like a familiar, comfortable arm around her small frame. That was the moment Sara looked over at them, bit her lip and whirled away. Blake followed her gaze, frowned at him and slammed back the rest of his beer. Rob was nowhere in sight.

"I created that mess." Suzanne's voice stayed low. "I loved him. A lot. But he…it wouldn't work. I felt like a predator most of the time. I seduced him, kept him at my house, it was…wrong. It totally fucked up our work environment even if he didn't want to admit it."

"But he loved you too." Craig surprised himself with this insight.

"Yes. It had to end. So... I ended it." She stepped out from under his arm. "You should go find her. She's in an incredibly tough place right now. Jack has a way of bringing out the worst in people."

To his utter amazement, she went up on her tiptoes and pressed soft lips to his before turning and walking towards Blake.

What in the hell?

He took a breath, and dove into the crowd, having turned into mostly a mass of people dancing to cranked-up tunes, to find Sara. His head swirled with a bizarre combination of sudden need for Suzanne's calm presence and insight and the intense desire to fix this thing for Sara.

Jack held his breath, let Heather grip his arm, as they ducked into the tent full of colleagues, lenders, title company flunkies, his brewery friends, and the one woman he wanted to see. He found her in a second, although she stood at nearly the opposite end of the blue and yellow tent. He swallowed hard, turned his attention back to his date–the woman he had to have a serious conversation with later, after the game. The scene she'd made in the club had solidified his resolve.

He was done.

"Don't drink too much," he muttered under his breath to her. She glared at him and sipped the bloody Mary someone had handed her, tightening her grip on his arm. He sighed, grabbed a soft drink, looked up and locked eyes with Sara. Raising his glass, he smiled, using every ounce of self-control he possessed to keep from shucking off Heather, running over to Sara, picking her up and carrying her out of the loud, annoying place.

She turned away though, chatting with someone he didn't recognize, so he refocused, reminded himself he still had great seats to what promised to be an amazing football game, and tucked his hand in his pocket. Heather looked up at him but kept her hand on his bicep.

Within an hour, anxiety buzzed so loud in his brain he could hardly stand still. He'd shaken Heather off at some point, and stood alone among the sea of people, unable to locate Sara anymore.

Get a grip God damn it. You know what to do. Dump the crazy bitch; go to the game, then get Sara back.

Yeah. Easy as that.

He rolled his head around, released some tension in his neck and sipped the beer he'd been nursing, wanting to keep his wits about him if at all possible. Hiding behind a buzz of alcohol had become too easy. He had to get control of himself. Then, he could control what happened next. He'd slipped, badly, after Sara left him. He'd allowed himself to coast back into bad habits, including the tall, dark one who was getting drunk off her ass over by the vodka and Red Bull bar.

A commotion by one of the beer bars caught his attention. Before he knew what happened, he'd made his way there, and stood in a strange tableau with the woman he loved yelling at her brother to leave her alone and to let her live her life, while her current boy-toy remained opposite the scene, staring daggers into his chest. Suzanne appeared at Craig's elbow, whispered in his ear, and seemed to calm him down.

Now that is a strange turn of events.

He watched the blonde man take a step toward Sara and felt something rise in his chest, making it impossible to breathe.

Mine.

He took his own step into the fray, catching Blake's eye, but stopped when Sara moved away from her brother and held out both arms. "Dear God, all of you, leave me alone. I don't need this right now. You," she pointed at Blake, "mind your own fucking business for a change. And you," She glared at Craig, "stop trying to convince me you know best. And you," Jack crossed his arms when her eyes met his. "You—just, oh hell." She dropped her arms and walked out, leaving an empty void between the men, who stood staring at each other.

Suzanne put her hand on Craig's arm, whispered something in his ear. He nodded and started after Sara. Jack felt the possessiveness smothering him again but had no interest in a pissing match with the guy. So, he squashed it best he could, and watched while Suzanne put an arm around Blake's shoulder. Glancing around he realized Rob had left the tent completely, and made a mental note to find out what the hell was going on with him and Sara's brother.

Jack turned and headed back into the crowd, ignoring everyone around him, seeking the bright yellow cap she wore. Determined to find her and try to calm her down, all the while a small voice inside reminded him that she didn't want to be helped. She'd said so herself. But he knew better.

Sara pushed blindly through the drunken group, let herself get buffeted, hugged, and ass slapped. Holding back tears, she wrenched free of the hands clutching her, suddenly unable to breathe another minute in the tent.

Air. She needed air.

The opening at the far end promised sunlight and freedom; she made a beeline for it, sucking in huge gulps of oxygen. If one more person touched her, gave her advice about her life or even looked at her she knew she'd scream.

Escape.

Shoving aside the tent flap she stumbled out into the bright, October sunshine then dropped into one of the chairs nearby, putting her head on the table. Her heart would not stop pounding. Finally, she sat up convinced she might live through the next few minutes when her eyes landed on a pair of folded hands boasting a French manicure. She sighed and met Heather's eyes.

"I know you're talking to him. Every night."

Sara stared, unable to process how completely insane her life had become. Heather took her silence for agreement.

"So you can just stop right now. He's with me, do you understand? You had your chance." Heather stood, wobbled and nearly fell. Sara watched as if from a long way away when the crazy bitch pointed a finger at her. "He's mine. He may talk to you every night but he's in my bed, *every* night." The woman gripped the back of the chair for balance as the level of her voice grew. "He tells you things he doesn't mean. You can't trust him. He doesn't miss you. He has me!" The last was loud enough to silence the small knot of people sitting at nearby table.

Sara closed her eyes, unwilling to engage on any level as her chest tightened and her head started ringing. She started at the touch of a hand on her shoulder. Looking up into Craig's dark eyes, she realized he'd been standing there, heard everything. She stood and nearly got bowled over by the man himself, rushing out of the tent opening.

"Can't you control her?" She glared at him as he gripped Heather's arm and led her away without a word, then slumped back into the chair. The pure, raw energy of jealousy thrummed through her body.

Recognizing it is half the battle, eh Sara?

She groaned and put her head back down. *Don't do it. Don't give in to it. You do not need either of these men. Walk away.*

The words her mother had said had worn a groove in her brain. "It's love Sara." She watched Jack's broad back as he walked away from her, and tried to quell the sudden bout of shivering that enveloped her.

Craig sat, put a hand on her shoulder then removed it. Images of her, of them together, swirled around in his brain, but the sudden new image of the petite redheaded woman intervened, making him grit his teeth. "You're right." He said to Sara's bowed head.

"About what?" Her voice muffled.

"We can't do this anymore." He stood, heart heavy. "I love you Sara." She sniffled, looked up at him.

"No you don't. You love the idea of me not with Jack. There's a difference."

He frowned, anger crowding out the confusion clanging around his psyche. "Don't tell me how I feel." He hauled her to her feet and kissed her, shoved his tongue between her lips, hands fisted in her hair. She responded at first, molding her body to his, making small sounds in her throat that ramped up his determination even further. The sound of a whistle broke the moment.

"Get a room kids!" She gasped as he gripped her face in his palms.

"I do love you, Sara, goddamn it, and it's killing me seeing you like this but…" he looked up, unsure how he felt since thoughts of Suzanne had begun to invade his dreams more and more.

She shook her head, tears streamed down her face. "Go. Leave me alone. I mean it Craig, I can't," she yanked herself out of his arms. "I can't do this anymore. It was a mistake, you and me. I, oh hell I used you, *used* you do you understand? I am still using you and it's not fair." She clutched his biceps. "You deserve better than me." He stared at her, resentment taking a firm foothold in his gut, but he knew he'd been complicit in the whole thing. .

"Yeah, I knew you were, though. I let you. Friends with benefits. Christ. Guess I'm just not cut out for that." He shrugged out of her grip and took a step back. Running a hand through his hair he caught a glimpse of Suzanne, still standing with Blake, their heads together in some kind of earnest conversation. A thrill of something he'd later identify as lust went through him at the sight of her but he repressed it, refocused on Sara. "You're right, like I said. We can't do this anymore. I am falling for you, period, "he sighed and shrugged.

She sat back down. "Yeah. Me. I'm a mess. Seriously Craig, let's just cool it, okay? I need space to think, figure out what the hell it is I really want."

He took a breath, forced away the intense urge to hold her, kiss her, to make it better. She smiled at him, nearly melting every bit of resolve in him. "You do deserve better." She put a hand to his face.

He moved out of her reach, lest he do something stupid. "Okay. Fine." Frustration surged through him like a wave, making his throat ache. "I'm going home." The band around his chest tightened when he got another glimpse of her deep green eyes, haunted and hurt. He'd be damned if he'd let that asshole do this to her. But, he had tried, and she still didn't want him, she wanted the asshole.

She stood, side stepped him and took off away from the loud party in the tent. Craig watched as she disappeared over a hill of the golf course where thousands of tailgaters made merry, sighed and ducked back inside. His heart ached as he caught Suzanne's eye. She leaned on The Local's bar; Blake had disappeared.

"I'm sorry honey, don't make me leave." Heather kept her death grip on Jack's arm even as he whistled for a passing taxi.

Jack bit back the urge to smack her on the ass, hard. She'd misinterpret it anyway so it would be wasted effort on his part. "Get in the car Heather. I'll pay the guy. Go home and sleep it off. I'm going to the game. Afterward, I want you to come over and clear your crap out of my house, do you get me?"

She jerked out of his grip, stumbled, and then righted herself. Jack kept a hand on the taxi door. His head had never been clearer. Heather turned to him, her face set and eyes wild.

"You don't love her you know. You just want what you can't fucking have. She knows that. She's playing you like a goddamned violin. Don't you get that?"

He kept his face neutral. "You're drunk. Again. You and I are through. Now get in the car."

She wrapped her arms around his neck. "Jaaaaack," her lips captured his but he turned away, pulling her arms off him, disgusted with himself for ever even touching her. "Honey, I'm sorry." He glared at her.

"Heather, I'm done. Get in the car now." She sniffled, slid into the back seat, tugging him down with her. He knelt by the open window.

"You won't be happy with her Jack. You're too much alike. You and me, we're better." She clutched his hand, tears streaming down her face. "I get you. She never will. Don't kid yourself."

He jumped up, avoiding the closing window just in time. He shoved his hands in his pockets and watched the yellow car weave into the increasing traffic around Michigan Stadium.

Heart light, head clear and laser focused, he turned and strode back towards the tent.

Sara.

He had to find her. Now.

Taking long strides, he calmed his breathing, trying to figure out what he could possibly say any differently to her than what he already had, but determined to try harder. By the time he got back to the tent, it had cleared some as people had made their way into the game. Sara was nowhere in sight. He grabbed a beer and slammed it, patted the inside pocket where he'd stashed his flask of bourbon and made his way into the nearly one hundred thousand people headed into the football game, figuring the distraction of a decent football game, and a solid, slow drunk would help.

He found his seat in the middle of a bunch of fellow realtors, laughed, joked and tried like hell not to stare around for her. The bourbon warmed him as the afternoon cooled down and the teams took the field. A sudden flurry of activity towards the aisle made him look and come face to face with her as she made her way down the row, apologizing along the way, only to plant herself right next to him.

"Hey." He handed her the flask. She took it and helped herself to a healthy slug.

"You're welcome." The crowd around them cheered as Michigan drew the first blood, scoring on their first drive down the field. He took the usual rash of shit from everyone around him and then leaned into Sara's ear. She sat stock still, staring straight ahead.

"Earth to Sara." She glared at him, but he kept his gaze neutral. She softened and slumped a little so he put a friendly arm around her shoulders. The sensation of her leaning into him felt more perfect than anything on the planet.

The crowd around them got more raucous and they laughed and chatted with colleagues and friends. At one point he looked at her, caught her staring at him. He glanced at his phone and noted what had to be the millionth text from Heather.

"So is this us, on a date?" She grinned and whispered in his ear. He realized the bourbon had loosened her up considerably and took the last sip just before the halftime show.

"Oh God no. Not us." She put a hand on his thigh, making his skin prickle in anticipation. He plucked it off, and put it back on her lap.

"Don't." He smiled at her and some perverse way got a thrill of satisfaction at the frustration that passed over her face.

"I thought we were sort of communicating well, you know, lately." Her voice took on an icy edge.

"Yeah, maybe, but I've got a huge fucking mess to deal with tonight, dislodging Heather from my place. Sorry. I'm distracted."

"Fine."

Her hand made its way back to his thigh as the game got exciting and when Michigan made a dramatic touchdown in the final seconds she leapt up and hugged him in her excitement. The very feel of her nearly made him keel over with a sudden surge of possessiveness. That fucking kid had been dipping into this, he knew it. He had to grit his teeth as raw jealously coursed through his veins.

As they made their way out, joining the throngs at the corner of Main and Stadium, she tucked a hand into the crook of his elbow. Using every particle of self-control he had, he moved away from her. "What, Jack? You're gonna stand there and tell me you didn't enjoy that? I mean, it was fun. I thought," she stared at him but he held his tongue. She set her shoulders and crossed her arms. "Well, do you want to walk back to my place?"

The look on her face, and the pure need that oozed from her made his body clench with intention. He clamped down on it. He did need to sort the thing out with Heather. Sara needed to sort out some shit in her own head. He turned to her once they were clear of the crowd on the sidewalk. "As tempting as that is, I'm gonna say no." It took all he had but he kept his distance. "I don't share and I won't ask you to. I need to clear things with Heather. And you," unable to resist, he tucked a thick curl of her hair back behind her ear. "You need to figure out what you really want."

"I really *want* you to come home with me Jack. What part of that didn't you get?"

He grinned, and brushed her lips with his, then leaned into her ear, taking a deep breath of her scent. "The part where you still have the dashing hero, Mr. Robinson, in your life." He walked away, hands in his pocket, heart in his throat before she could say anything else.

Sara watched him go, her entire body thrumming with residual energy and quickly fading happiness. As the reality stole over her–that he'd told her essentially to let go of Craig, to choose one of them or the other–sunk in, and irritation replaced the pleasant glow of the time they'd just spent together.

Asshole.

She grabbed her phone and dashed off a text, telling Val to meet her at Café Luis downtown for a martini then headed in the opposite direction from her condo, diving back into the teeming hoards of football fans exiting Michigan Stadium.

Fuck him and his pompous ultimatum. She'd do this thing on her own terms, not at his command.

CHAPTER FOURTEEN

"C'mon honey, let's find you a cab."

"But, I want…" Sara signaled the cute waiter who'd slipped his number to her on a napkin.

"Nope, no more. Let's go." She focused briefly on her friend. The room spun then stopped as she attempted to look more sober than she actually was. Val stuck her in the backseat of a taxi, then crouched down by the open door as Sara tried not to gag at the old cigarette and cheap leather odors. "Sara, you have got to get this thing sorted out."

She nodded, felt a tear slip down her cheek but didn't wipe it away.

Val patted her leg. "I'll call you tomorrow. Do you want me to let Jack know…?"

"No!" Sara glared at her, tried to focus on her friend's face. "I'm fine. I don't need babysitters. I mean, sorry, I don't mean to be such a bitch. Don't tell him anything. I'll be fine." Val shut the door and Sara closed her eyes, opening them when the car stopped in front of her condo.

After paying and making her wobbly way up the sidewalk, she nearly stumbled over someone on the steps. She glared at the masculine hand on her arm, keeping her upright. "What the hell?"

Craig's face became clear, sending a bright shaft of annoyance through her brain. She yanked her arm out his grip. "What do you want? I told you I need some space."

He took her keys and unlocked the door without a word. She took off her jacket and scarf, and then kicked off her shoes before stomping into the kitchen for water. The light nearly blinded her, but she sucked down two glasses before turning to acknowledge the man's silent presence behind her.

"Why are you here?"

"Just wanted to make sure," she cut him off, as the extreme emotion of the day and the grip of two stiff martinis washed over her, drowning out reason.

"Christ, Craig. Why don't you get a grip? Stop being so fucking....nice all the time." She moved past him, but gasped when he grabbed her arm and pulled her close, his lips hovering over hers.

"Okay." He said, simply. Then slanted his mouth over hers, shutting out all sensation but for his hands and lips.

Craig had spent the last weeks in a wash of frustration and anger. The fact that Sara had been ignoring him did not help his mood. As the youngest of five boys he'd learned to be quiet, to watch, listen and learn and not let his emotions lead him. But something had built in him since first encountering Sara, something that felt wild, uncontrollable, possessive and competitive all at once. Not a healthy way to feel about a woman he knew. The longer he went without actually talking to her the worse it got. It made him antsy, quick tempered, and pretty much miserable and he'd wanted to skip the whole fucking tailgate party altogether.

So, when drunken Heather had broken the news that Sara and Jack had been talking every night, he'd practically been frozen with fury. The exchange he'd had with her after that had simply not been enough. They needed....something. Closure. So he'd headed to her place, waited, and now in the face of whatever shit she was slinging, he lost it. Completely and utterly lost it.

He fisted hands in her hair and swept into her mouth with his tongue, pressing his body into hers. A brilliant beam of need, anger, frustration and something a little scary lit the edges of his vision. The small sound of pleasure that she made in her throat egged him on, driving to say things, do things he never believed himself capable of. Her shirt ripped under his hands and he watched it drop to the floor as if seeing it with someone else's eyes. He felt her fumble with his zipper, free his rock hard shaft, sensed her hand on his flesh as he tugged her away from the sink and pressed her up against the kitchen wall.

"Nice, huh?" He yanked her jeans and panties down, growling into her neck, biting, sucking. "I'll show you fucking nice." She groaned as he plunged his fingers into her pussy, reaching high, stroking her clit at the same time. Her nipple contracted in his mouth, and she lifted her hands over her head, letting him finger fuck her, bite her, which somehow made him even madder. His cock ached, and his head roared, deafening him as her lusty scent enveloped them. Her pussy clenched once, twice and she came, hard, crying out his name and threading his fingers in his hair. He pulled his fingers out and stood, staring at her, fisting his own cock, trying to sort through the nauseating swirl of emotion in his gut. "Turn around," he growled. "I need to fuck you."

She opened her eyes and stared at him, meeting his anger with her own and then dropped to her knees. She swallowed his cock, and cupping his balls in one hand while drawing her other one down his chest. "Oh Jesus," He groaned, and tilted his hips bracing his hands on the wall behind her. He shoved his cock down further, fucked her mouth until the orgasm hovered just out of reach. "Stand up god damn it."

She wiped her lips and covered his mouth with hers, giving him a taste of himself, before she turned and presented that luscious ass to him. "Do it then." She whispered. "I want it."

He stopped, ran both hands from her shoulders, to her waist, and clutched her hips. Settling his cock into the cleft of her ass he sighed, realizing he'd become something he didn't like but couldn't stop now. It felt too god damned good. Without warning, preamble or another word he shifted, and slid into her depths with one long stroke. Keeping one hand on her ass, he reached up and fisted her hair, tugging her head back as he pounded into her. The amazing clutch of her pussy and the sounds of her moans brought him back to the edge, made him come up on his tiptoes and grunt with the exertion of not coming.

"What are you waiting for? Harder!" She pressed back, meeting his thrusts. He saw her reach down with one hand and tease her own clit. That did it. He gripped her hair hard, knowing it had to hurt but unable to stop and fucked her so hard he saw stars as the climax roared up from his spine and enclosed him in a dark space before exploding behind his eyes. "God! Yes!" His hips kept moving, as his cock released and released and she pressed back, her pussy spasming and pulsing along with him, pulling him ever deeper, towards what he had no idea.

Finally, when he thought he could speak coherently again, he pulled out and released her hair. The anger still made him feel brittle, unwilling to talk. She glared at him and walked out, presumably towards her room without a word, leaving him standing there, clock still hard, glistening, head still pounding. Good Christ, what a mess. He tugged his jeans back up and sat, trying to regain his equilibrium.

The whole thing–the push and pull, this or that, will she or won't she he'd been through made him ill. He had to stop it now before it killed him. He put his head in his hands, then stood and followed her into the bedroom, smiling at the sight of her, naked and lying face down on the bed. If Jack could see her now….he grimaced at himself, then eased her under the covers before climbing in himself, as far from her as he could get and still be in the same bed.

Sara woke with a start, confused, head aching and mouth dry as a bone. After ascertaining she was naked and there was someone snoring next to her, she panicked and crept into the bathroom, the familiar ache between her legs one of the only clue she had about what had happened. Flashes of drunken memory–her kitchen, Craig, his lips, cock, rough, harsh words. Tears pressed against her eyes. What had she done? What had she said to him?

She cleaned up, brushed her teeth and tried not to puke up the water she gulped down in a no-doubt too-late attempt at hydration. After determining the liquid would stay in place, she tiptoed back to the bed. "Sara?" She nearly jumped out of her skin but quelled the urge to tell him to get the hell out of her house and merely got back under her covers. She jerked her shoulder away when he touched her, embarrassed, unable to remember completely what had happened. God that hadn't happened to her in years. Tears dropped onto her pillow as Craig eased up behind her, pulled her body against his and brushed his lips along the back of her neck.

"Stop it." She muttered. The unmistakable feel his erection made her want to scream with frustration at herself. A hand cupped her breast; fingers pinched her nipple, making moisture slicken the tops of her thighs.

"No," he growled in her ear and reached down to touch her clit, then slipped a finger inside her, making her jump and moan. "I'm not gonna stop. I am gonna fuck you again. And I think you want it, don't you?" She sighed, arched her back and let her body take over, let the once gentle, tender man take her again, rough, demanding and exhilarating, shutting out the clamor in her head. The voice that haunted her days and nights. The one that spoke one man's name.

Sara groaned and pulled a pillow over her head, trying to force the exquisite hangover agony to cease. It didn't help. She rolled onto her side into a ball. Maybe if she got really, really, small, it would mistake her for someone else and spare her. No luck. The sickening pounding in her ears matched her heart and the sunlight sliced like a knife between her eyes.

She dragged herself to seated, put a shaking hand over her face before having to lie back from dizziness. Bad idea. Nausea rushed up, forcing her from the bed and into the bathroom. After about ten minutes of losing everything in her stomach, and likely in the stomachs of all her former lives, she sat huddled on the floor, wishing for death. She groaned and pictured her calendar, realized she had exactly two weeks to go until her period.

Yeah.

Great.

She rose, ducked under the shower and scrubbed off, rationalizing away the distinct possibility that she could be pregnant. By a man she was very likely using to forget another. She dried off and dressed, smiling when she heard Craig's laughter, the lilt of his drawl, and realized his must be talking to someone back home. He always went full Southern when talking with people who had accents.

His words stopped her dead in her tracks, the brush frozen over her wet hair.

"Yeah, yeah, I beat the bastard at his own game this time."

She frowned, hoping she didn't hear that or at least had misinterpreted it.

"No, fair and square. The best man won, in a big way." She dropped the brush with a clatter. *What the fuck?* She leaned out, knowing she shouldn't eavesdrop; it would only make it worse.

"Of course it's a contest." Craig moved around her kitchen. She heard coffee pouring, the sizzle of more bacon hitting the pan. "Everything is with him. But, I held fast, had my plan, implemented it and viola. Here I am!" He laughed again. "Of course I had a plan. You have to when dealing with a guy like that."

Sara's knees wobbled, she slid down her bedroom wall, hand over her eyes. *A contest? With a winner? And a prize. Yes, indeed. A prize.*

Holy shit. She'd been played?

No, no, calm down. He's just...what? Gloating about winning her?

Rage rose in her chest so fast she couldn't breathe. Gulping and sputtering, she got to her feet and marched across the living room into the kitchen. The bastard stood there, towel around his waist, back to her, too-long hair damp from a shower.

"Oh, we'll see I guess. But, rest assured, he'll be hearing from me. It's not a worthwhile win unless there's....huh?" He spun around when she tapped his shoulder. His smile seemed so natural, unreal for a guy who'd just been caught bragging about beating Jack at the "win Sara" game she didn't even know they'd been playing. She could barely hear as the roaring in her ears drowned everything out but the sound of her own voice.

"Leave. Now." She crossed her arms.

"Hang on a sec." he frowned at her. "Why? I don't have to be there until…"

She grabbed his phone. "He'll call you back." She said, ending the call for him. "I heard you. Congrats on winning me. Now get the fuck out of my house." He gaped at her, and then nodded, smiling.

"Oh, honey, I wasn't…" She sidestepped him. Men and their infernal excuses. She had no more time for any of it.

"I'm not kidding Craig. Get out. I don't ever," she gulped, as the tears let loose. "I don't ever want to see you again."

He stood back, hands on hips. "You don't know what you heard Sara. Don't be so stubborn. Let me explain at least."

She held up a hand. "Don't even try." Using every ounce of resolve, she left him standing there, slamming the door of her bedroom for good measure before flopping down on the bed and letting the sobs rip through her.

Craig's jaw ached from clenching it, cursing himself for what he'd done, and left undone. Driving on autopilot, he found himself sitting outside the large, imposing bungalow belonging to one Jack Gordon. He'd been there once before, back while Sara and Jack were still officially together, for a poker night with "the boys." He'd be the first to admit it had been fun. The guy knew how to throw a party even of that size. Staring at the porch light that still shone and a light sheen of frost that tipped the perfectly mown grass of the large front yard, he sensed his wildly beating heart finally slowing. What in the hell he thought he'd do now, he had no idea, but the longer he sat, the calmer he got. The buzz of his phone made him jump, and scrabble down into his jeans pocket for the thing.

"Hey," Suzanne's soft voice on the other end made him close his eyes, regret, embarrassment and anger at himself nearly bowing him over.

"Hey, yourself." He ran hand across his rough jaw. "What's up?" They had been talking a fair bit, easing ever closer to something resembling a date, but Craig kept holding back, not even sure why. Until that moment. He spoke before he could talk himself out of it. "Can I come over?"

"Uh, sure, I'm not exactly…"

"I don't care. I need to talk to you."

"Okay, I'm at one nineteen Barton Drive," she named one of the most exclusive streets in one of Ann Arbor's old-money neighborhoods.

By the time Craig got there, he had nearly backed out of the whole thing, but the sight of her sitting on her massive front porch steps, a small redheaded figure holding two cups of coffee, lifted his heart. He popped a mint into his mouth and got out, leaning on the truck door a minute. She held up one of the steaming mugs.

"I look like ten miles of bad road, sorry." He made his way up and took a seat next to her. She smelled clean, fresh. He took a deep breath. "I have been a real shit in the last twenty four hours."

"Yeah, Jack has a way of bringing that out in people. Don't know why. He really is a nice guy." She leaned into him, making him feel better and worse at the same time.

"Oh, I don't think I'll blame him for this one, Suzanne." He took a sip and watched a squirrel make its way across her lawn. "I, um, she…oh fuck."

She patted his knee. "Take your time."

He took a deep breath. "I'm over her. I think." Suzanne kept quiet, sipping her coffee and staring out into the yard. "But I was a complete shit to her in the meantime. And now I have to leave town for two weeks."

"Don't be so hard on yourself. She'll calm down. She's like her brother that way. They fly off the handle, then spend about a day calming down."

"No, I was really not a nice guy." He put his empty mug down on the step and stood, shoving his hands in his pockets. She pinned him with her deep blue gaze, making his skin pebble a little. Her smile made his shoulders relax.

"Maybe she needed that. I mean, she's pretty damn conflicted right now. You didn't help, being such a nice guy and all." She leaned back on one elbow, never breaking eye contact. He couldn't move. His heart started pounding again. With his own action, he probably had driven her right back into Gordon's arms. Suddenly that didn't seem like such a bad thing.

The craziness of the past months passed through his brain in a montage. Her lips, hands, laugh, sarcastic sense of humor; everything about her that had driven him for so long, started to fade as he watched the slight figure of the woman still sitting at his feet. He reached out a hand and pulled her to standing. She remained on an upper step, nearly at his eye level. She put a hand on his shoulder, the other against his cheek.

"Some people are just meant to be together, Craig no matter how much we might think otherwise. There is no explaining it. I for one, think those two are just such people. And I never, ever thought I'd say that about my friend Jack." Her smile faded, her face took on an almost regretful look. He suddenly felt like a double shit. She'd probably thought the same thing about the man she'd married; the man who'd given her this mansion of a house, and then dropped dead one day from a rogue blood clot in his brain. Without thinking, he pulled her into his arms.

"You are amazing. I'm sorry to dump this on you." She leaned back, then into his ear.

"It's okay. You're pretty amazing yourself." The sudden touch of her lips, soft against his, brought a flush to his whole body. He made himself stop, cradled her face in his hands as he spoke.

"I don't think…" she put a finger to his lips.

"Sometimes you shouldn't think," but she just gave him a quick squeeze before letting him go. "Have a safe trip. Call me."

And, with that, she turned and ran back into her house without another word. Craig stared at the place where she'd just been, amazed and a little unnerved by the fluttery sensation in his chest.

      After about an hour, a scalding hot shower and sips of weak coffee, Sara felt compelled to pull up the photos she kept on her computer and phone from her New Year's vacation with Jack. The photographers had strolled around constantly, snapping pictures you could purchase. Jack had scoffed, kept ignoring them, but when presented with the proofs at checkout, he'd been speechless. She recalled looking over his shoulder at the screen, scalp tingling, as she saw the moments captured between them. She bit her lip, scrolling back through scenes of dinners, sunbathing, on a catamaran for the day. But, the one that had made him purchase the entire lot of them still had the power to leave her breathless.

      They sat together on the beach, the sun rising behind them, Sara with her arms and chin resting on her knees and a small smile teasing her lips. Jack had an arm around her shoulders and eyes fixed on her, lips near hear ear. She remembered what he had said right then too. She'd never forget it.

      "You are my whole life. And that scares the shit out of me."

      She shuddered, recalling that she'd not even answered him. Had been unable to process it. But the photo captured it, forced his voice deep into her brain. She shook her head. She had to erase it from her memory banks and that meant one thing. She swallowed hard, and hit the delete button, as a single tear slid down her face. It seared her nerve endings, nearly made her scramble down to the tiny garbage can icon to retrieve them. But, it had to be done.

      She regained her composure and went on a punishing run in the cold afternoon. The mental and literal purge of the men who'd haunted her life for over a year felt good, but not great. The ever-present sting of loss when she realized she couldn't reach out to call Jack that night hurt like nothing she'd ever experienced in her life.

Her eyes lit on the embossed deep black invitation to the downtown building opening party. November eighth. The day she would be married. Now it was the day she'd face him, once and for all, in the building they'd worked so hard on, that represented so much of their months together. Wiping her eyes, she stood, still holding the invitation, and wandered into her bedroom to sleep off some of the overindulgence.

CHAPTER FIFTEEN

Sara stood in the office break room a few days before the big party; the no one could stop talking about, sipping coffee and staring at the sales board. Squinting, thinking she must be seeing things, she saw the words: 1515 Hill Street, a plum office building listing next to "Craig Robinson." Her hands shook as she put the coffee mug down on the counter. *Holy shit. That was Jack's listing.* They'd been talking about how to market it the week before the tailgate, brainstorming the various businesses they knew who could put the beautiful old building to best use.

The words: "I beat the bastard at his own game," and "you don't know what you heard, Sara," careened through her brain so fast she had to take a seat. Her phone buzzed with a text from Jack.

"Did you like how the invites turned out?"

She smiled at it, finally realizing that she knew what she wanted. That last strange night with Craig had sealed it for her. She didn't answer the text.

He'd been sending texts, emails, and calling. By then she'd become expert at Jack Gordon avoidance and knew what he meant anyway. She'd designed those invitations with him, nearly six months ago. She looked up at the sales board again and then sent a text to Craig, who'd left for Louisville with plans for a mini vacation back home before his brother's wedding.

Two words.

"I'm sorry."

She sent it, then, feeling better than she had in ages, went about the busy day ahead.

During that week, she ran twice a day to keep her head clear, didn't touch a drop of alcohol, and got plenty of sleep every night. She closed two of her biggest transactions in her career up to that point as well. The amount of the commission checks astounded her, but she channeled Jack and put enough aside for taxes and the rest in her Roth IRA. The irony that he exercised positive control over her still, in spite of her resistance, made it tough to pass on the glass of wine, but she pulled on her running shoes instead.

Try as she would, the man would not leave her thoughts. She decided she'd go to his party, the one she'd help him plan all those months ago, and corner him to talk, really talk. It scared and exhilarated her at the same time, and she determined not to lose her nerve–to have this long-in-coming chat once and for all. Ironically, on the very weekend they would have been married.

By Thursday, she felt strong, alert and in control of her emotions enough to handle, what she knew would be a high-powered event. She'd had some late showings and pulled into her spot, already planning her evening of run, shower, salad and bed and nearly fell over Blake, who sat perched on her porch steps, beer in hand. She frowned, realizing he was already halfway to seriously drunk.

"What are you doing here? What's wrong?" She took a seat next to him.

"He left."

"Who?" But, she knew and her heart sank. "Oh honey," she put her arm around him. He grimaced and shrugged her off.

"Whatever. It's my fault." He put the empty beer bottle down and reached for another. She grabbed it out of his hand.

"Come inside. Let's get some water."

"Leave me alone."

"No, Blake. I'm taking care of you for a change. Now get the hell up and come inside."

He let her lead him in. "Jesus, it's clean in here." He glanced around before flopping down on her couch. "Can I stay? I can't face the house right now." Sara's heart broke for her brother as she watched a tear fall from under the hand he had over his eyes. She sat next to him.

"We suck at this, don't we?" He sat and sucked back the water before groaning and lying back again.

"At what?" He stared up at the ceiling.

"At love."

He snorted and turned on his side. "Yeah, I guess. What's with the extreme organization in here? Hire a maid?"

"No. It's Jack. Sometimes he brings out the good stuff too."

She stood and drew a blanket up over her brother's thin frame. "Stay, sleep it off. But, you have to talk to him. You guys can't…" Her brother held up a hand.

"Stay together anymore apparently."

"Don't be silly Blake. It's a temporary setback. Get your head on straight and work it out with him. You know you want to."

"Big talk from the queen of non-commitment." Instead of making her mad, the comment made her smile.

"Not for much longer. Now sleep."

The week had provided enough stress and extra work to keep Jack on his toes. Unable to sleep, with details and last minute dilemmas swirling through his head, he usually gave up and drove down to his building – project he'd birthed, babied, and bullied from concept, to purchase, to fruition over the past year. He would forever associate it with the craziness that was his relationship with Sara. Doing mundane chores like fastening towel rods to freshly painted walls and installing light fixtures in the middle of the night brought him incredible peace. He'd even stayed in one of the empty condos a few nights, waking confused and sore from sleeping on a too-short couch.

But, he had a plan. Every day brought him closer to the one thing he now knew without a doubt he wanted. No detail of the massive party went un-sweated. Nor did the details for the penthouse flat he had outfitted for her. The one he planned to take her to the night of the party, to prove what he wanted, and get her to come to her senses.

They were meant to be together. He merely had to show her.

The Friday before the event he'd been in a sleep-deprived haze, but knew between him, Jason, and the new girl he'd hired a few months ago specifically to implement this party, everything would be absolutely perfect. He took the day off, did his usual ten miles in the November cold and collapsed in bed after a long hot shower, having spent the night before putting the finishing touches on the condo, ordering the finest champagne and making sure the florist remembered to add rose petals to his huge order of arrangements. By midnight that night he'd taken one last look at the place, large four poster bed with restraints, spanking bench and the box containing a new ring, one not so flashy and over the top, more in keeping with how he felt. Solid, sure and willing to prove he could be trusted; an emerald nestled between two diamonds, set in an art deco swirl of platinum.

Perfect.

He'd smiled, and flipped off the lights.

While he slept that day, dreams of Sara, her voice, hands, lips, laughter, eyes, and body that he knew so well flowed in and around his subconscious. By the time he awoke, he had a raging hard on to take care of, then showered and donned the new tux he'd had tailored for the occasion. He gulped down anxiety at the thought she might resist, without a single worry about the event itself. The party would be flawless and he'd have the place rented and sold within weeks. At least he felt confident about that.

He arrived as the caterer started setting up the tables in the back of the cavernous first floor retail space. The band had already set up. His friend Evan stood around watching as the bar with its ten taps and stainless-steel top was assembled, rolling his eyes when Jack arrived.

" 'Over the top' is your middle name, you know it Jackie-boy?" He smiled and slapped his friend on the back. "I gotta go change. See you in a few hours."

Jack answered a few emails from his phone and watched as the well-planned event unfolded around him. He sent out a single text:

"Looking forward to seeing you tonight" to Sara, then rose and made a final pass through the room, making sure everything was ready for the big night.

CHAPTER SIXTEEN

Sara gazed at her image in the full-length mirror. A black, form-fitting dress with a halter-style, neckline plunging slightly in back, and a slit up the side to the middle of her thigh hung perfectly on her reflection. For this party she treated herself to this little number. She had spent the afternoon getting her hair put up and having a full manicure and pedicure at her favorite nail bar after running six miles in some pretty cold temps just to work up her nerve to attend the thing.

Her phone buzzed with a text. Craig. Her faced got hot as she read it. He had not responded to her first apology but she knew he'd gotten it.

"I'm certain you'll be the hottest woman there, and we know what that does to certain colleagues of ours. I'm not saying don't have fun Sara. Just be careful. Guard your heart. It's important to me."

She sighed, put the finishing touches on her makeup and squared her shoulders. After applying Chanel to her neck and wrists, she added simple diamond studs to her ears, suppressing the memory of last Christmas, when Jack had hidden them under her pillow, and slid her feet into sexy four-inch suede pumps. A strange beat of excitement played through her body as she climbed into the taxi.

She would have fun tonight goddamn it. She hadn't been dancing in ages. All of her friends would be there. Blake even claimed he'd show. After a couple of days alone, he'd gotten less frantic and had promised her he'd be talking to Rob soon. She chewed the inside of her cheek nervously. Images of the one man she wanted to see kept swirling through her brain, making her forget the carefully practiced words she wanted to say to him.

Acutely aware of the bare state of her skin under the hot dress, she closed her eyes against the memory of his voice.

Yes. You want him. Tonight you could get him, you know; if you'd just let yourself own the power you have.

Yes, she knew what Jack liked all right, and figured he'd know exactly what she wasn't wearing the moment he saw her. The thought of tormenting him felt sweet but wrong at the same time. *Focus. This is about talking. Starting over, even, if it's not too late.*

The front of the renovated red brick building glowed from about a million small white lights and luminaries lining the sidewalks in both directions. The awning over the front door and a doorman in full uniform, opening car doors for people to walk across a short span of red carpet made her smile. Sara heard strains of Vivaldi softer and louder in time to the door's opening and closing, as she eased out of her taxi, took the doorman's hand and allowed herself to be lead to the door.

An attendant took her coat and her bag. Several friends immediately accosted her from other offices, laughing and pointing out the incredible features of the cavernous space. They went up about five open steps to an enormous room that was floor to ceiling windows, just slightly above street level. Sara admired the familiar fifteen-foot ceilings, exposed mechanicals and ductwork, cork floors. A full bar temporarily dominated the huge room, with real beer taps behind the twelve foot long gleaming counter. Young women and men in white jackets and, in the case of the women, short black skirts and high heels wandered in and out of the crowd, carrying gourmet morsels for sampling.

She smiled to herself. They'd spent lots of late nights perusing plans and talking through various risky scenarios. The fact that he'd actually gone with the most dynamic of the plans, the one she'd advocated, made her ears ring. She tried not to look around too obviously for the man of the hour.

"Christ, what in the hell makes him think anyone would rent this?" Blake asked appearing at her elbow with a perfectly mixed gin and tonic in hand. He looked rested and calm, to her relief.

"Don't be a cynic," she demanded. "It's amazing, and you know it."

"Ok, so this practically unusable but sexy space is one thing–what's upstairs?"

"Two types of condos–lofts and two bedroom units, all with front or side facing views," she sipped the drink he'd brought her.

"You look great tonight." She glanced at him, hoping her nervousness wasn't too obvious.

"Thanks. Rob here?"

He raised an eyebrow at her. "Yeah, he's coming. We are working things out I think."

She put an arm around his waist. "Thank God. You guys are my touchstone, you know? Giving me faith in coupledom."

He snorted. "Well, so what's up with you and our host?"

She sighed and leaned on his shoulder. "I'm a mess Blake. Can you fix it for me?"

He kissed her head. "Nope. But at least you admit it's a mess. That's half the battle isn't it?"

She watched the well-dressed crowd ebb and flow, wishing for just a glimpse of him. Then berated herself for needing that. Blake leaned into her ear. "He's right over there." She started, pulled away. He smiled, and kissed her cheek. "It's okay Sara. I get it."

Blake turned around to point out a knot of people gathered in the center of the room. An older woman, at least fifty and incredibly classy in a slim cream pantsuit was leaning back as Jack spoke, a slight smile on her lips. There were about seven people gathered around, chatting, but mostly listening as Jack gave his spiel.

"She owns the rights to the Urban Outfitters franchise in this region. Jack is about to close that deal for this space. He is such an incredible prick, but he could sell an Eskimo an ice cube, huh Sara," he laughed. "And the man can throw a party."

She took one last look at him at him and turned away to mingle, and caught up with Jennifer Stewart, who gave her a warm hug.

"Well if it isn't my favorite Stewart Realtor," Jenny said to her, as she smiled and held her at arm's length. Sara finished her drink and set it on a passing tray held by one of the beautiful hired helpers. Several other colleagues joined them. Greg walked up and put his arm around his wife's waist.

"Yes, my dear, agents like you are the future of our company, no doubt." As he spoke Sara's skin started tingling. Jack had broken away from his conversation with the potential tenants, and moved towards them, but stopped to laugh, hug and kiss the many women who reached out for him. Sara rolled her eyes, and tried like hell to calm her suddenly racing pulse.

"Whew," he wiped his brow and shot his cuffs. "The gauntlet has been run. What do you guys think? Good party, eh?" He grinned at the group in general, avoiding Sara's eyes.

Blake was at her elbow again, with a fresh drink in one hand. She leaned into him, grateful for his support.

"I was just telling Sara that it's professionals like her, and like you, Jack, that are the real future of our business," Greg slapped the taller man on the back and moved away, already having a new conversation with a different group.

"Sara, good to see you," the warm hand on her back made her skin pebble. She stared straight ahead determined not let her body react, not to succumb to the pure chemistry that swirled between them. Images of the photo she'd deleted flashed in her vision, along with an epiphany. In every single photo she loved from their amazing New Years' vacation, either Jack or she was intent on the other. Never once did their eyes meet. Every one of those pictures reflected exactly what was wrong between them. They never met half way; never gave as much as they got. But their late night chats, where they opened up and really talked, had given her strength. She straightened up, realizing this was neither the time nor place to get into it.

"Nice event Jack. Well done." She meant it but realized nothing short of perfection would do for him.

A weight settled in her stomach. She should leave. It was a mistake to come here. He looked so amazing in that tux, complete with black shirt and tie, classy, understated. She had to clench her fists against the impulse to slip her hand into the crook of his elbow as he worked the room, doing what he did best. Her resolve to talk slipped a little further beneath the haze of lust and physical need she figured she must have been wearing like a "Hello my name is" sticker.

Jack had made a quick perusal of the general environment around him, as any good host would, making sure food and alcohol flowed, and people kept smiling and laughing, enjoying themselves. This was his element, truly, and he had even been able to ignore Sara once he realized she'd entered the place, at least until now. She looked like a million fucking bucks in that dress. The line of her neck sorely tempted him, exposed and elegant. He shoved his hands into his pockets and kept talking to the people all around him, his brain on autopilot.

He knew, just as he knew his own shoe size, that she had nothing on underneath, just as he liked it. When she took a step away from him, he mirrored her. Buttoning his jacket to hide his reaction to her, he spotted Suzanne and Evan across the room. "Save me a dance," he whispered, and escaped before he grabbed her by the hand and dragged her upstairs. He suddenly had a vision of her working the party with him, as he knew she could. His desire for that nearly overwhelmed him. As he made his way across the crowded room, he reminded himself of tonight's goal. Reinforced his determination to finish this night the way he had planned, which meant he couldn't tip her off too early to his eagerness.

"I have the retail space seventy-five percent rented, but give Jason a call tomorrow if you want to discuss the basement." He tossed the comment over his shoulder, responding to a question about availability, as he moved quickly away from her.

Sara drained the drink in her hand, laughed, and moved from group to group, accepting their kudos at her recent successes, aware of how the men watched her breasts and her ass which were hugged just so by the clingy material. She played it up, touching their arms, and smiling as if whatever stupid shit came out of their mouths constituted the cleverest statements she'd ever heard.

When she looked up her eyes met his. She swallowed the lump that had risen in her throat. How the hell did he do that anyway? He could anticipate every emotion, every small nuance of mood and the electricity crackling between them now set off a small flame of sheer lust in her core. She looked away, frowned and plunged back into the crowd that had grown and gotten steadily louder, drowning out the string quartet that played in one corner.

Sara grinned into a fresh drink, recalling the argument they'd had over music. He hadn't wanted the live performer's expense but she insisted and he must have stuck with that plan. Something made her look up. Jack held up a glass across the room, and stared straight at her. *Damn.* She looked away. *How did he do that?*

Shaking her head at herself, she made her way over to the bar. Jason stood, beer in hand, observing the room. "Nice work." His face twisted into an ironic smile.

"Yeah. I'll be glad when it's over. But the party planner did a good job."

Leaning back against the stainless steel bar top she tried to relax. Jason perched on a chair. They watched in comfortable silence as the crowd grew, and the musicians packed up their instruments. The rock band members had arrived and the transition would be quick, ramping up the vibe to true party level soon. "What happened to doing this last week? You guys were ready, I know you were." Jason shot her a strange look.

"Jack changed it. Cost a fortune to re-print the invites I can tell you." He leaned close to her ear. "He's been a machine lately. Don't know what's up with you guys but…"

She moved away. "There is nothing up with us, Jason. You know that."

He shrugged. "Maybe there should be. He's going nuts Sara, honestly."

"Not my problem," but the hand holding the drink to her lips shook. She did not need this right now. "Oh hell," she caught sight of a tall, thin woman with jet black hair break loose from a group and head straight for. "What now?"

Jason put a hand on her shoulder. "Don't worry. I've got your back." She rolled her eyes at him then faced Heather, the one woman who had seemingly stood in the way of her happy ending. She looked nervous, but determined.

"Look, Heather, spare me another reminder about who owns Jack, okay?"

The tall woman took a deep breath and gripped Sara's arm, startling her. "I'm sorry, honestly. Can we talk a second?" Sara glanced at Jason, who shrugged and moved into the crowd, leaving them alone. A tingling in her scalp signaled Jack's eyes on her again. She looked across the room and saw him, frowning at the sight of the two women standing together. He raised an eyebrow at her. She mouthed "it's okay" to him before turning her attention to the tall brunette with her long fingers clenched together. She opened her mouth speak but Heather beat her to it.

"You have to get back together with him." Sara closed her eyes. *What in the hell?*

She reopened them, leveling a stare at the woman.

"Changed your tune fairly significantly. What happened?"

"He needs you. You need him. I was just a distraction. I get that now." She slid into a bar chair, her face a mask of misery. "You two should be together. It won't be easy but he's worth it and you know that. He's," Sara held up her hand as words she didn't really mean rushed past her lips as if in self-defense.

"It's over between us Heather."

"But you have to give him a chance. He needs that. It's part of why you're so perfect together." She stood. "He'll do anything for you, why can't you see that? Are you that stubborn?" Sara opened her mouth, but no words came out. "You are about to throw away the best thing that could happen to you. He's not perfect, but no one is. Give him a chance. You won't be sorry." Tears glinted in the woman's dark eyes.

Jack appeared behind her, and Sara's skin prickled in anticipation of a scene. Heather turned and gave him a hug, whispered something in his ear and walked away. He stood, hands in his pockets, within two feet of her, but as far as Sara was concerned, on the other side of a chasm suddenly too wide and deep for her to breach. Even talking to him seemed futile. The intensity was too much. She should escape while she still could.

Jack's entire body buzzed and every nerve ending danced with need as he kept himself separate from her. "Sorry. Hope she didn't upset you."

Sara touched her hair. He felt the nervousness and anxiety pour off her like a wave. *That crazy bitch. Leave it to her to mess up his plan.* Sara smiled, keeping her distance from him. "No, she's fine. Pleaded your case for you, actually. Cute."

"Oh, um, okay." He blinked and tried to convince himself the other thing he picked up from her mirrored his own thoughts of pure, unbridled, need. He gulped, then recovered. "So, good call on the music." She laughed, sending chills down his spine. He curled his hands into fists, kept them hidden in his pockets. *Keep it casual, for now.* "I think you'll like this band too," he nodded toward the stage where the group of guys and one girl prepared to perform. "Can I get you a drink?"

She kept her eyes on him, making him nervous with the intensity of her stare. "No, thanks. I'll, um, just go see…" She gave up and dropped onto a barstool. "Why are you doing this?" He moved closer, letting his body take over then clamping down on the urge to kiss her, an urge that pierced him straight through the chest. His vision darkened, the room went quiet in his ears as he zeroed in on her lips. Suddenly he knew what he had to do. It was not a simple matter of playtime later. He had a harder job, one that would prove his intentions for the long run. He sighed, touched her lips with a finger. She shivered. "Go away, Jack. Work the party. Leave me alone."

He turned without a word, lest he risk acting like a complete idiot. The word "headspace" flittered through his brain. He'd done it before. Taken a woman right to the edge of pleasure again and again, making her so completely satisfied with words and action she'd been a limp ragdoll for hours after, and had gone completely nuts begging for it again. He took a breath. He knew her so well; he could make that happen, but it meant an even deeper plunge into his role. One he likely would have a tough time giving up ever again. He looked around, spotted Evan chatting with members of city council at the other end of the bar and headed over to him, needing his advice once more.

Sara watched his broad retreating shoulders and fixed her mind on resistance. She had to. It couldn't be any other way with him. No matter what anyone said now, no matter that Blake even seemed to think it inevitable. She would not go there again with him. The dialogue she'd imagined between them, the way they could ease back into their relationship, seemed ludicrous and naive to her. She couldn't handle it. Didn't want to, at the same time, she wanted nothing more.

She let Greg Stewart drag her onto the dance floor as the band launched into their first set. She stayed there for a solid forty-five minutes, doing her best to avoid the one man she wanted, needed, to see again.

By the time she'd broken a sweat and danced with three or four different guys, she realized every single song the band covered, were ones she had on her playlist. She laughed, raised her arms, let herself go, and caught his eye again. He stood at the bar with his friend Evan. The other man seemed to be worried about something, his mouth moved, talking intently to Jack while he stared straight at her, eyes dark and searching. She winked and turned, shook her hips probably more than was necessary, but no longer caring. She wanted to have fun goddamn it and he could take his obsessive whatever and stuff it. She needed some release from the buckets full of tensions she'd been lugging around with her for months now.

The band took a break and she let one of the guys from her office tug her over the to bar. She slammed back some water, keeping her gaze on the guy running his mouth next to her, unable to hear him, or feel anything but raw need for the man across the room.

The room had narrowed to two people as far as Jack was concerned. He had planned this thing weeks ago, but had spent the past ten days or so working every last detail. He made small talk, flirted, and pretended to drink knowing he'd require his wits about him later, all of the usual, while aware of exactly where Sara was in the room the whole time. She moved around, doing her thing, unaware of what he had planned for her. Evan had been skeptical, even worried that taking Sara that far tonight meant nothing but potential trouble.

"She's not ready for that man. Seriously." Still, he'd given Jack a few tips, a pat on the back, and a sincere wish good luck.

Jack put his glass down on a passing tray and looked up to see Greg Stewart frowning at him, cigar clenched in his teeth.

"Hey Greg," he muttered as he watched some tool tug Sara off the dance floor and monopolize her in a way that set his teeth on edge. "What's up? Don't you like the stogie?"

"Yeah, I do, thanks," Greg growled at him. "What I don't like is what is going on with you and my new superstar over there. You know, the hot one in the black dress?"

Jack pulled his eyes away from her and stared at his broker.

"What are you talking about?"

"You know exactly what I'm talking about Gordon. Pam made me come over here and tell you to leave her the fuck alone."

"Well, if I remember correctly, if you and your wife had your way, I'd be her manager right now," Jack stated. He wasn't about to take personal life advice from Greg Stewart. He'd lucked into a wife who put up with his fucking around for years before he got too old and too fat to appeal to anyone else.

"Yeah, well good thing you passed on that because that would be one mess I would not want to untangle. She cut you loose once. Can't you take a hint?"

Greg put a hand on his arm.

"Look, Jack, you have no reason to take advice from me." Jack kept watching Sara flirt with the guy across the room. "We're just worried about her, and I don't think you should mess with her anymore. Just my two cents."

They both turned an observed Sara a minute in silence. As Greg walked way, Jack grabbed a drink off a passing tray and drained it. He'd not been drinking much at all in the weeks since the football game and the two he'd had so far were going down way too fast. He snagged water and held onto it trying not to look as conflicted as he felt.

Sara begged off from the next round of dancing, needing to hydrate some more and found herself standing next to Adam, Mr. Floor Fucker with a Fiancée.

"Hi Sara, you look amazing tonight," he said leaning over to kiss her.

Jesus, Mary and Joseph, what next? She kissed him back, lightly.

"Well hello there," she said as she turned away from him, and finished her water. It was amazing what a year did. There had been a time when this guy had been the Next Best Thing in her universe. Now, he represented a moment in time she wanted back– the early rush of adrenaline as she and Jack got to know each other.

"….and so, I ended up rattling around that huge place on my own," she heard him say and she turned back and stared at him.

"I'm sorry, what did you say?"

"Oh, just that Lou ended up, um, moving away before, you know..." he trailed off and glanced around the room.

She shrugged. Figured. "Well, sorry about that." She moved a few inches away from him as the band switched gears into some more modern stuff and she felt a hand on her shoulder.

"May I?" Blake. She smiled at Adam and waved as her brother led her onto the dance floor. Within seconds of tuning to face him she locked eyes with the blonde woman who'd tried to insert herself as Mrs. Jack Gordon, the one whose house Sara had sold, bringing on this entire insanity with the man as far as she was concerned.. *Dear God, the gang is certainly all here.* She rolled her eyes as the woman zeroed in on the tall man standing alone across the dance floor.

The room's lighting changed. It got darker, more like a club with lights over the bar and from the street casing a glow over the band and dancers. The noise in the room escalated as the non-dancers carried on conversations over the live music.

Yet another one of her favorite indie rock songs blasted out from the speakers. Sara broke away from Blake and danced alone for a moment before Jack appeared in front of her, his presence sucking up the oxygen in her space. She moved nearer, warning bells clanging in her head, but her body warming, getting lighter as he danced with her. He had an unselfconscious rhythm, matching hers, not too over to top but not the bogus shuffling so many less-confident guys adopted on the dance floor.

They'd hit some pretty great nightclubs in St. Bart's. Sara grinned at the memory. He'd made her play a game with him there. Pretend they didn't know each other, let him pick her up, work for it a little until they slammed the bathroom door shut and he fucked her up against the wall. Her face heated up, matching the slow burn in her core.

They didn't talk. Just danced, and danced. Sara felt sweat pooling between her breasts but her hands stayed ice cold. She suddenly needed to get away – to escape Jack's inevitable, unexplainable pull. She held her hands up.

"Break time," she stated and started to turn away from him before she made a fool of herself by jumping into his arms.

"Wait. One more song." He tugged her back as the band launched into a popular country rock duet with the male and female lead singers.

He released her to let her spin under his upheld arm, and then pulled her back, laughing, as they moved together two-stepping to the country beat. She couldn't ignore his eyes, deep midnight blue, as he moved with her, and she reveled in the oh-so-familiar strength of his arms under her hands. She sensed the eyes of the crowd on them as the song ended and she remained in his arms, her hands behind her back, not allowing herself to touch him but leaning back and looking up at him as his hands ran up her bare back, setting her skin on fire.

Jack started, sensing someone next to them. Suzanne stood there, a hand on his arm.

"Next dance for me?"

"Uh, sure," he forced himself to take his eyes off Sara. "Hey, short stuff, you look fucking hot–why don't you wear that to work? I'd be by more often," he took a deep breath and re-focused as he watched Blake lead Sara towards the bar.

He mentally pictured the room again. The one where he'd take Sara to a place in her head she would love, but could also hate at the same time. He smiled at Suzanne, held her close as they danced to a slow song, giving her a squeeze at the end. Jason waved frantically from across the room so he made his way over, counting minutes now that it approached eleven. He had to get her upstairs, soon, or he could possibly implode.

"Jack, the caterer's almost out of food. Do you want them to get more?"

He frowned at his watch. "No. Let's wind it down."

It was Jason's turn to frown. "Really? It's only ten forty-five." Jack ground his teeth.

"I know but I need this thing to end on time. I gotta get on with...oh hell you handle it. If you and the party girl think we need more food, you make the call. Consider yourself empowered." Jason lifted an eyebrow at him. Jack sighed. "Sorry. I'm just, preoccupied. Handle it. I'm gonna get some air." He shouldered past the blonde woman poised to grab his arm and made it outside, took huge gulps of the cold Michigan night. Keeping his hands propped on his knees he let the air calm his nerves. He knew upping the ante for Sara that night meant taking a lot of energy from him. But he wanted it and figured it was likely his last chance. He needed to make it meaningful. Needed to rock her so hard she'd realize how much she completed him.

"Jack?" Yet another party guest needing something. He groaned, and went back into the steadily overheating room filled with people dancing, drinking, flirting, and if were not mistaken, making out in the corners. He grinned.

Time to get on with the real party.

CHAPTER SEVENTEEN

Blake leaned back on the bar, his tall lover kept a hand on his shoulder, the conversation they seemed to be having one of intense emotion. Sara sighed and moved away, giving them a little privacy. The sensations from her body kept sending her distinct messages, ones she found harder and harder to ignore. She saw him re-enter the room, get waylaid by some other female who dragged him back out onto the dance floor.

"You're a grown woman, Sara, you can make your own decisions, but I just want you to know I'm here if you need me," Blake's voice surprised her.

"I know. I love you," she leaned on his shoulder.

The band gave its best Red Hot Chili Peppers imitation as "Give It Away" blasted out next. She grabbed her brother's hand and led him to the dance floor unable to resist, needing to dance to release some tension.

"Now for one more slow tune, before a break," the lead singer finally announced. Sara turned to leave the floor, but Adam found her and pulled her back. He had just started to speak when Jack put his hand on his shoulder.

"Do you mind, this is our song," he said pulling the other man off her with little effort.

She put her arms around Jack's neck, took a deep breath determined not to react. He pulled her close. The hand on her back heated her skin. He leaned into her neck, as she closed her eyes and moved to the music with him. His lips hovered around her ear, but never made contact. They didn't speak, but she could feel him, his lean strength painfully familiar, and her body started betraying her resolve.

She made an effort get her breathing under control. She found herself arching into his body, pressing against him, wishing he would pick her up and take her away from here, right now. Tears threatened behind her eyes as the song ended and she broke away quickly.

"Thanks, Jack, nice rescue," indicating Adam with her head and made her way to the bar. He followed her. She leaned forward on her elbows, Jack stayed in her space, leaning backwards facing out over the crowd.

Sara let the scents and sounds of the party wash over her. Nearly eleven now, and still packed, people moved to and fro, coming together for conversations and even a little making out in dark corners. Ceiling fans circulated the air, and blowing the wisps of her hair around her neck.

The sudden sensation of his lips on her bare shoulder, tongue lingering on her skin made her close her eyes.

"Stop it," but the weakness in her voice betrayed her words.

She sensed the party's pulse, as the crowd moved about her, some dancing to the canned music, laughing, drinking, talking, and yet felt as if she and Jack were in a weird bubble somehow removed from it all.

"Stop what," he asked, as he moved slightly closer to her.

She pulled her arm out of his range.

"It is a great party," she told him. "No detail left undone."

He shifted so that he leaned on one arm facing her, his breath on her neck, his torso so near she could feel the heat from his skin.

"We are an amazing team, Sara," he whispered to her. "Can't you see that?"

She turned to him, noting the scary proximity of his lips to hers.

"I don't know what you're talking about," she whispered back. Her nerves jangled then went silent, succumbing to his calm, letting him soothe in way she still didn't understand.

"Us, Sara," he insisted, "you and me, together. You heard Greg; we are the future of this company, this industry. We know how to own this business, and can only be better at it together."

He leaned in to brush his lips against her ear and she had to clench her fists to resist reaching out for him.

"The way you work a room, it's like I'm watching myself, you know? I love that about you," he whispered.

She pushed herself up off the bar, angry with him, with herself, with her own weak-kneed response to him. A tiny voice reminded her that she was as turned on as she'd been in weeks. She was moving towards him, and dancing away; knowing exactly how the night would end.

They stayed frozen in place. Jack not giving in to the loud requests for his presence on the dance floor, simply staring at her, hands in pockets, eyes blazing with something she didn't recognize. She could already feel his hands on her nipples, his mouth on her neck, although he was just standing there, looking at her. She heard his deep voice, telling her what to do, how to feel, to give in and trust him. She stumbled as a sudden claustrophobia enveloped her like a blanket. She stepped away from him and then panicked when he gripped her bicep.

"We could really be great together," he repeated. "I wish you could see that. I wish I had figured it out sooner myself."

"Let go of me." She couldn't take it another minute. "I'm going home."

He tightened his grip instead, slowly pulling her back, using his other hand to circle her waist. "I have something for you, upstairs." She shivered again, already agreeing in her head as her lips formed the words.

"I'm leaving."

"No, you're not." His breath heated her skin. "The penthouse condo Sara, meet me there in thirty minutes."

He released her and walked away, making her stumble again, not realizing she'd been leaning into him. She bit her lip. What a colossal egomaniacal asshole. But she already knew she'd go.

Just once more, New Sara justified to her. *One more time around the playroom with him. Then you leave. Forever.*

Jack took a breath, picked up a conversational thread with the city council twerps but kept a close eye on her. Bound and determined to make up for years of bullshit, dissembling and compartmentalizing with women, with her. He'd been completely serious when he told her he wanted her as a partner, in all aspects of his life. The sight of her fucking around with that damn kid for the past few months had driven him around the bend. She was his goddamn it. He needed to prove it to her. He had so much more to offer but wanted her alongside him, irritating control-freak that she was, and he smiled to himself, knowing he could pull this off, especially since Blondie had taken a powder tonight.

A calm settled over his brain. The relief at finally knowing the moment was near, all the planning done, gave him a different kind of a buzz. He shifted, buttoned his coat over the growing bulge under his zipper. It would be tough, but he'd prove it once and for all, to her and likely to himself. They were meant to be together.

He smiled, grabbed more water and worked through the crowd. He only had a few minutes to disentangle himself from this thing. Giving Jason a high sign, he made his way around the room, shaking hands, hugging women, his mind clear, his body revving into high gear. He watched her hit the up button on the elevator, and caught her eye as she looked over her shoulder. He took the steps three a time to beat her there.

By the time the elevator doors slid open, Jack already stood, a smile on his face and a blindfold dangling from his fingers. He tugged her out of the lift, pulled her close, walking her back until she had her back pressed against the wall outside the condo door. He held her hands over her head, and kissed her with a dizzy intensity.

"God, I have missed you," he said into her skin. She closed her eyes, determined to be the recipient of this, as Jack moved his body against hers. He allowed her to lower her arms around his neck, grasped her back with both hands, owning her with his mouth. She gasped when he broke away and held her face in his hands. "C'mon in," he whispered, touching her nose with his lips. "I've been waiting weeks for this." He reached behind her and turned the knob. Smells and sights assaulted her senses. Flashes of candlelight, a plate piled high with strawberries, a floor covered in rose petals, a bottle of champagne chilling on ice…and the spanking bench, restraints and soft leather strap hanging from the ceiling made her gulp. Jack's strong arm circled her waist, his lips tickling her ear. "Welcome." He pulled her to the giant bed, sat, pulling her onto his lap. She straddled him, her brain on fire and her body not far behind.

"Just this once Jack," her voice broke. "Then we're done. Do you understand?"

"Hmmm…we'll see about that." He pushed her up, ran his hands down her body, and then stood, burrowing into her psyche with his deep stare. He ran a finger across her lips. "Leave it to me. Deal?" She nodded, not trusting her voice.

He reached over for the champagne but bypassed it, instead taking a cube of ice and putting it against her lips. He smiled; let it trail a chilly line down her neck. She shivered, loving and hating the pleasure/pain of this, knowing it was only the beginning. "Hey!" she shuddered and jumped away when he let the cube drop down between her breasts. His grin nearly broke her in two. *Dear Lord she'd missed him too.* Something happened as she took the step between them, closing the chasm she'd created a few short months before. He grabbed her hand, brought it to his lips, sucked each finger into his mouth then pressed a kiss to her palm. She closed her eyes.

"Look at me Sara." His voice had a low grumble to it she recognized, and if she'd been wearing panties, they'd be damp at the sound of it. "I'm going to only say this once before we start. Before, our play was just that. I let you keep some control. Tonight will be different." She swallowed hard and started to speak. He put a finger over her lips.

"Shh…let me finish." He held her close, his lips close to her ear. "Tonight I'm in complete control. I will not hurt you, but I'm going to push you a little." His hand roamed down her back, cupped her ass. She gasped when he pressed into her, his need obvious, hard and urgent against the clingy, now irritating fabric of her dress. "Ready?"

She nodded and he released her, but didn't touch her again. She ran a nervous hand up her arm, started to unlatch the halter top. He put a hand on her then, nearly bringing her to her knees with lust. "Stop. Let me." He flipped it open with one hand; she let the dress drop to the floor. "Oh yes. Perfect." He cupped one breast, ran his other hand down her hip and back up. "Leave the shoes on." He took her hand and led her to the strap hanging from the ceiling. When he tugged her arms up she started to resist.

"Jack, I'm…I'm scared." Her lip trembled. An unwanted tear escaped down her cheek. "Not of this," she jerked her chin at the paraphernalia. "Of you."

He smiled, slipped out of his jacket, and without word, keeping his gaze locked on hers, pulled her arms up, fastening her wrists in the buttery soft leather. She shivered as he ran both hands down her arms, slanting his mouth over hers, possessing her with his lips and tongue. Her pussy responded, sending zings of pleasure shooting through her body. "Oh God," she gasped when he dropped to his knees in front of her, pulled one of her legs over his shoulder. "I'm, oh Jesus, Jack," she tugged at the restraint, the leather making a creaky sound tightening as she squirmed. He sucked her clit hard, making her hips buck against him. It hurt, and was, at the same time, the most exquisite feeling on the planet. Just as the room lightened around her, the climax roaring up from her core, he released her. She could hardly catch a breath, watched as he reached for a strawberry, dredged it through the cream and held it to her lips.

She opened her mouth, but he kept it out of reach. She could smell it, the heavy richness of the white coating the deep red strawberry. He grinned, popped it into his own mouth, but before she could whine he had another one, had it pressed to her lips. She bit into it, letting it drench her senses, the cream running down the side of her mouth. He leaned in and licked it from her neck, but forcing her leg down when she tried to wrap it around him.

"Nuh uh Sara. Not yet." He took the champagne bottle and took a drink right from it, held it to her lips and smiled as she gulped at it. One more strawberry followed, fat, bloated and delicious. Sara had the immediate sensation of drowning, in his eyes, his voice, wanting more than anything for him to kiss her again. "Kiss me. Please?" She whispered, licking her lips as he released his cufflinks and rolled up his sleeves.

In a blink, he was at her mouth, teasing, licking, tracing the line of it with his tongue but staying out of reach. She whimpered, but he kept at it, teasing, letting his palms flit over her enervated skin, bringing every nerve ending she had to strict attention.

The room lightened again, got fuzzy around the edges.

Then he was gone once more, leaving her gasping. A blindfold covered her eyes. A rich cinnamon, gingery exotic scent filled her nose. "I know you don't like this." His voice hovered at her ear. "The blindfold. I need you to wear it. Give over to your other senses." She felt his fingertip trace her neck, across her collarbones, to one aching nipple then the other. It reached her stomach, then lower, making her groan when he reached her pulsing clit, pressing there, then even lower, filling her, stretching her body, making her shudder.

Then, as her groans filled the room, he stopped. No lips, no fingers; nothing on her. She took a deep breath; let the waxy, sweet, rich combination of smells roll through her brain. Hands gripped her hips from behind, slid up to cup her breasts. Cool metal joined them. "Oh Jesus!" she cried out as one of her nipples received the clamp. A low moan of pain escaped her lips.

"Use the word, baby, if you need it."

She shook her head, taking deep breaths and grunting low in her throat when he fastened her other nipple between the clamp's jaws. Her pussy pulsed, her brain buzzed and a crazy sensation of quiet enveloped her. The soft music he'd been playing, the trickle of a waterfall installed along one wall, all ceased as if a switch had been flipped. All she needed, all she wanted to hear was his voice.

"Jack?" Her voice cracked.

"Right here baby." He tugged at the chain connecting the clamps, making her hiss and squirm. His lips found hers again, and she let herself fall into him, letting him carry her over some invisible line. His fingers found her clit, flicking at it, giving her pressure then releasing, before he slipped fingers inside her dripping wet pussy, reaching high, aiming right for her sweet spot.

"Ah God, Jack!" She yelled, anxious and yearning for the release he kept promising.

"Mmmm….no, not yet." He pulled his fingers out, and she tasted herself when he put them to her lips. She sucked hard, thrilled to hear his breath catch, the soft satisfied sound he made.

Then nothing, again. Utter silence descended. She knew he'd left the room, could sense his absence as keenly as his presence. Her skin prickled. The bite of the clamps seemed to disappear. But she didn't cry out. Knew she didn't have to. He'd be back. He'd always be back. That realization took hold, made her suck in a breath.

He would always be back. She sniffled, wriggled her wrists so she could feel the leather against her skin.

The sensation of calm, of ease, of completeness settled around her nerves. When his hands grabbed her hips, she cried out. *How in God's name could she be comfortable like this?* But she was. He made her that way. He ground his still trouser-covered hard cock against her. "I need you," she whispered, "so much." Hands fiddled with her hair, pins dropped to the floor as he released it, letting it flow around her shoulders and down her back. Fingers threaded through it, pulling some, rubbing her scalp. She sensed him move around to her front. One hand stayed in her hair, pulled her head back. She moaned when his lips found her neck, sucked and bit her skin.

"I know you do. I'm here. I'll always be here for you Sara." He said in between bringing her close to orgasm again without even touching her anywhere but her hair and neck. Her hips thrust forward; her clit ached, needing contact. He cupped her mound with one hand, the heat of his flesh providing just enough pleasure to make her moan as she moved against his palm. "Oh please Jack. Please I need to come."

"No. Not yet. You have to wait." Fury rose in her brain.

Who the hell did he think he was, toying with her like this?

He covered her lips with his, sweeping into her mouth with his tongue, tangling both hands in her hair now. His kiss spoke to her, reminded her of his role. He mastered her but she didn't have to worry. He'd be there. Always. Tears slicked her face and she tasted salt on his lips.

"Ready?" He asked. She nodded, not knowing what came next only that Jack had her, and he'd never hurt her or let her be hurt. She groaned when he unclamped her nipples but let out a scream of shock when he pressed ice cubes to her abused flesh. The amazing absence of the pain, the intensity of it, then its fade as her body adjusted, made stars flash behind her eyes. Pleasure and pain shot through her, making her whimper and bite back the urge to beg for the clamps back in some perverse reversal of need.

"Holy shit, Jack that's, ahhh." He licked her neck, kept both hands on her aching breasts.

"Shh...relax." His voice oozed into her psyche. The room got loud again, the music and the waterfall sounds slamming into her brain, making her whimper. A strawberry appeared at her lips and she bit down on it, let the juice drip down her neck, groaning when he licked it away. Then nothing, again. He was gone, leaving her body pulsing with energy and need.

Sara knew she hovered at a precipice. She could make a choice. At that moment, her body craved release but her brain had settled; her nerves no longer jangled as they had been doing for weeks. The rough sound of his voice, the touch of his hand, just the looks he'd been shooting her all night had brought her to that moment. She took a breath and let it take her, let her body fully relax for the first time in months.

As if he sensed her giving way, he held on tight from behind, cupping her breasts, then moving down to tease her clit and pussy again, never staying in one place long. "I think we need one more thing, don't you?" He must have shed his shirt at some point and the delicious sensation of his flesh against her back made her sigh, and arch her hips. He put a foot between hers, shoving his thigh against her pussy. She moved her hips, ground against his leg, needing to climax so badly she wanted to cry. She did cry, could hear herself sobbing; could feel the tears slip out from under the blindfold.

"Arch your back Sara," Jack commanded as he pushed one leg away from the other, forcing her legs apart.

Panic shot through her. The moment she'd been attacked last year came swirling through her brain. She tugged at the restraint over her head.

"No, I can't. I'm scared. My feet are getting numb. I can't–I can't feel my hands. Jack." Her voice sounded breathy, anxious, but her brain kept pouring some kind of calming elixir over her nerves. It had to be the strangest sensation in the world. Abject terror, white-hot fury, and a clean pure jolt of need warred in her. Then nothing. Crystal clear calm made it all the turbulence, all the chaos of her last year fade into nothingness, like it had never happened. She tasted her own tears.

"I know. Give it to me. Let me have it." He bit her neck, ran a hand across her ass. "Give it to me Sara." She winced when his palm met her flesh, the smacking sound echoing around in her ears. "It's mine. All of it. Your fear, hate, anger, love – it's mine. Give it to me." He smacked her again, then once more, harder. "Come. Now." Her body obeyed even as the astonishing tranquility poured through her psyche. Fluid coated her thighs as she moaned, cried his name, but couldn't hear herself. Her words slurred and her vision darkened behind the blindfold. The orgasm plowed her under, made her whole body release energy from the tip of her tingling scalp to her shaking toes. She slumped, letting the leather hold her up, pull at her sore shoulders.

"Jack, please I need you inside me." Those were the words she tried to say, but they made no sense, garbled with some strange intense emotion she had no name for, as her entire universe narrowed to a pinprick of light, then winked out. At the center of the dark hallway he stood, arms out.

"I've got you baby. I'll always have you." She sobbed and slumped against him.

Jack couldn't breathe. His chest ached and his eyes burned. His woman now. He knew her best and her worst, and wanted it all. Her moan, cries, and bone-deep orgasm nearly brought him to his knees. When she slumped against him he flicked the restraints open, caught her in his arms. The beast in him roared, beat its chest, dimmed his vision and heightened his other senses. He could smell her, her juice, lust and release in every pore. He felt her skin, wet, hot all over as he kissed her. Primal need flared, his cock leaked and throbbed. He'd already come once. He'd had to leave the room to wipe himself off. *Sweet Jesus, what a fucking buzz.*

"Jack," she muttered against his neck as he held her on the floor, smoothing her hair back, letting her utter submission to him infuse his soul. "I'm not scared anymore." He smiled, picked her up and laid her on the bed. Starting at her feet he found every inch of her flesh with his lips and tongue, dipping into her dripping pussy, lower, loving the beautiful pink rosebud of her ass, then working up, dipping into her bellybutton, lapping the sweat from between her luscious breasts, then finally up the long line of her neck to her lips once again.

He allowed himself a moment to feel her sex pulse against him before he entered her body with one firm thrust, groaning as she enveloped him, gripped his cock. "Fuck me hard Jack. I need it." She gasped but he slowed, wanting to relish it, take his time. Her body spread, taking his girth, pulsing, tugging him straight over the cliff.

"Sara, I won't last long baby."

"Fill me Jack. Please, give me what I gave you." Her eyes were bright. As he lowered his lips to hers, she brought both legs up, giving him a better angle. He pounded into her, groaning into her mouth, their bodies dancing toward release together. The orgasm flashed bright behind his eyes and his hips thrust hard again and again, the smell of their combined lust swirling around him.

"Ah God!" He grunted, and his body tensed before releasing. A glorious shaft of pure pleasure ripped him in two. The gut deep climax kept up, his hips kept pumping, filling her body, fulfilling a primal function as old as time. She gripped him, held on, and cradled his head to her breasts.

"I love you Sara. So much. I, I need you in my life. Please. Please stay with me."

CHAPTER EIGHTEEN

Sara had never felt, in all of her nearly thirty years, so content. So utterly sated and happy. How he had done it, she had no idea. One thing was certain, all the signs and signals, conversations and long nights awake, wishing to be in his arms again, lead her to this exact moment. She had found her man and she'd do anything to keep him. He sighed, slipped out of her and collapsed down on the bed.

She stretched, went up on an elbow and watched him, saw the familiar signs of his body easing out of one mode and into another. She ran a finger down his stubbled jaw. "Wow." She smiled when he raised an eyebrow at her.

"Master of the understatement, aren't you?"

"Don't laugh Jack. That was…just…wow. Can we do it again?"

He tugged her to his chest, pressed kisses against her hair. "Sure baby. Any time you want." She sat, rolled her arms to work the soreness there and wandered into the fully stocked bathroom.

She stared at herself a minute. *Sara, you have done the exact opposite of what you told yourself. You let him do this, manipulate you, control you.* She shook her head, shutting down the negative noises inside it. *It's what I want.* She declared to herself.

No, it's what I need. She washed her hands, passed them down her body. She felt full, complete, and ripe. A stab of fear iced its way into her consciousness, thoughts of bad timing and a distinct lack of condoms making her dizzy.

She held back the panic fluttering on the edges of her horizon. No, she was safe with him. She knew it now. Still…letting herself go like that had been terrifying, exhilarating and now made her heart pound with residual anxiety. She needed him again, badly. But she forced herself to stay alone a minute. Gather her wits.

She bit her lip, decided to keep that detail about "bad timing" and "no condoms" out of the pillow talk for now. When she went out the bed was rumpled and empty. Following the sound of his voice she found him in the kitchen, naked, drinking from the champagne bottle and talking on the phone. He handed the bottle to her and finished talking to Jason, giving him final orders about wrapping up the party. She wrapped a hand around his magnificent cock, grinning when he pulled the phone from his ear and groaned.

"Okay, we'll, um I'll be back down in a few. Buy you a night cap." He dropped the phone on the counter, and lowered his lips to hers, kissing her with passion, intensity and emotion, leaving her breathless and wanting more. "Baby, keep that up and poor Jason will be stuck waiting for me another hour." He moaned and cupped her breast. "But if I'm not mistaken, I think I forgot to give you something." She frowned when he moved back into the bedroom, returning with what was unmistakably another jeweler's box.

The ring was magnificent; fit her like a charm. She swallowed, nodded and wrapped herself around him. "Mine." She heard him mutter into her neck. He released her, ran a finger down her cheek. His next words made her chest constrict. "No more blonde boy toy? I win this round?" She glared at him, shrugged out of his arms. Alarm bells rang loud and clear in her clearing head.

"What did you say?" A sudden tightening in chest made her gasp. She tried to keep her voice light, but felt herself shutting down again, letting go of the exquisite clarity he'd brought her earlier.

He tried to pull her back but anger deafened her, made her dizzy, breathless. She stomped back into the bedroom and pulled her dress on. She'd done it again. She'd let herself go; this time farther than she ever had. Let him release all her fears and … and… dear God. She sank to the floor, covered her eyes. He tugged her to her feet, but she pulled away, had the ring in hand already.

"Nice try Jack, really. A for fucking effort. You don't *win* me. I…."

His eyes darkened. "Goddamn it to hell and back woman did you not hear anything I said? Did I not give you what you needed? Christ almighty!" He ran a hand through his hair. "I *love* you. Can't you believe that? I don't think you're a prize to win. I'm…oh hell." He stepped into his pants, found his shirt and shoved his arms into the sleeves. "You are impossible."

Sara felt the last bit of her heart crack into a million pieces and fall to the floor. His eyes snapped with fury, then he dropped to the bed, put his head in his hands.

"Come home with me tonight. I need to wrap this place up; we could get some real food, talk. Let me explain. Something?"

She allowed him to hold her hand in his, but shook her head no. He stood and pulled her to him, crushed her up against his chest, leaned down to kiss her but she turned away. Her mind literally spun, coming down off an amazing high of the long sexy build up to their connection; but she was starting to panic at the thought of Craig, her brother, her friends

"Jack, I have to go home. I have to think about this," she said firmly. *Get a morning after pill.* "This was not a good idea, you know? As good as it felt," she whispered into his neck, still smelling passion on his skin.

"I've given you space Sara. I can't play that game anymore. You need me, you said so yourself. Why do you let such stubborn bullshit get in the way of your happiness?"

She shrugged him off, suddenly furious and him and at herself for being so weak.

"Excuse me, but no one can make me do anything. I wanted Craig, and we had a lot of great times together, that was my choice. I came here tonight knowing where your head was about me." She couldn't stop, the words spilling out hurtful and unforgiving. "Maybe *I* played you…I have *some* control here," she insisted, her fists and teeth clenched in anger. She held up her hand to stop him from interrupting. "You came here primed to force me back into this very position but maybe I was controlling you, did you ever consider that? Maybe I just wanted to get laid, nothing more. I knew you wanted me, after all." She could hear own voice, rising, louder, hating herself for getting into this crazy emotional state, but unable to stop.

Her soul screamed at her to stop, to listen, to get back to that crazy space in her head where she knew nothing but Jack, knew only that he would never leave or hurt her. But that moment was gone, vanished with the blink of an eye, the slip of conversation, when he revealed why he'd done all of this – to "win." It made her crazy with fury, willing to say anything to hurt him.

Jack could not believe this was happening. How in the hell had he gone from "yes I will marry you" to "I'm not a prize to be won?" Dear God but she could be aggravating. His mouth formed words before his brain fully engaged. "Oh, yeah, I get it now. You wanted to fuck with me for some payback over the Heather thing, so you got it. Great. That's just great. Nice work," he turned from her. "Couldn't have played it better myself."

He stood facing the window, then squared his shoulders, tucked his shirt into his suit trousers. *Nice work. Some Master you are, Gordon. Fucked it up yet again.* Words tumbled from his mouth, not stopping by for a reality check in his brain.

"I guess you learned a little bit from me during our hot summer, eh, Sara," he smirked at her, his self-confident, self-satisfied regular expression firmly in place once again. His heart ached, but maybe she had it right. Maybe there was a bit competition in all this but God help him, he did love her. "I mean, you got real backbone, some serious confidence since the first time I fucked you against the wall that night in your office. Do you remember that night?" She turned her back on him, stomped into the kitchen. He followed her.

"You can't take all the credit for blowing the doors off at Stewarts the second half of the year, I don't think, " he stood up to his full height, taking a deep breath as if reluctant to say what next came out of his mouth. "Yep," he ran both hands down his chest in a self-congratulating fashion. "You got some of that old Jack Magic, right from the main source. Hope it won't dry up for you now, since you've decided to turn into a raving bitch," he declared.

Jack could not process what came from his mouth, sick about it, but unable to stop now. His natural instinct for self-preservation clicked firmly in place, making him say things he really did not mean, in the interest of keeping her aware of who the fuck was in control here. He couldn't stop, despite the look in her eyes, a look that promised but didn't deliver.

"And to think just five minutes ago you were offering me a ring and a sleepover," she said sarcasm dripping from her words, "and all that money on the party, too. How much did you have to pay the band to learn those songs they'd played to push me into your arms?" She folded her arms over her chest. His head pounded with frustration. "Fucking sucks when you can't control absolutely everything doesn't it?" she spat out. "You have *no* control over me and you did not give me anything this summer except one deal that almost didn't close. I earned maybe five bucks an hour on that one and have you to thank for it. The rest of it was *mine*, all me, you fucking self-centered asshole," she finished, arms now down at her side, fists clenched.

Christ in a sidecar, he wanted her again. Her temper, her honestly earned outrage, he fucking loved that about her. She took shit off no one, not even him. He decided to give it one more try. He took a step towards her, gripped her upper arms, and brought his mouth hard down her hers. She tried to turn away but he persisted, clutching her face, forcing her to turn back to him.

She pushed against his chest, shivering, as the sweat had cooled her body temperature and emotion had cooled them both. He kissed her, and kissed her, holding her tight until he felt her give.

He broke away abruptly, stared at her, eyes narrowed, teeth clenched, breathing fast, as though wishing he could say something that would stop the arguing. He couldn't imagine what she was thinking but had the sudden distinct impression that her cruel words were a shield she had erected around herself. His knees nearly gave out when he grasped once again their eerily similar defensive mechanisms.

She still had control issues but he could deal with that. His gaze dropped to her chest that heaved in anger, kissed her lightly on the top of her left breast, ran his hands down her sides, to her waist, and put his hand on her belly for just a moment.

Then his brain shut down. The intensity of the night was too much to bear. He couldn't do this. He wouldn't do this. Fuck her and her goddamned independent streak. She could keep it.

He stepped and touched her face with one hand, drew his fingers down her temple, her cheek and cupped her chin in his palm.

"I made you, Sara," he said softly, his soft tone belying the cruelty of his words. "You are a Jack Gordon creation, don't ever think otherwise, but I don't begrudge the creative process – you are incredibly hot, can fuck with the best of them, and I've enjoyed making you come, watching you emerge as a confident, sexual female – a white hot sales professional," she pulled her face away from his touch. "I can recommend an emergency room for the morning after pill; I've had a little experience in that department as well." He stepped away from her.

The sound of her palm hitting his face echoed in the nearly empty room. Blinding fury tore through him, but he didn't flinch, just took the blow and looked at her as blood rushed to his skin. She had her arm raised to do it again but he grabbed her wrist and leaned into her so close he could smell the sweat, sex and pure female of her.

"Oh, no, the creation turns on the creator, what a shame," his eyes narrowed. "I guess you'll have to find your inspiration elsewhere from now on," Their faces were mere inches apart. "You'll never have this again, Sara, sure you want to toss it away?" He let go of her wrist, leaving her arm up in the air and he made himself smile, keeping it wistful.

He deserved the blow. His need to protect himself had overpowered him; had taken over and made him say some of the most ridiculous shit. *He wanted her, why couldn't he just admit that?* Too many years of lies and denial, he guessed. Reaching out to her as she leaned into him after his last crazy tirade, hoping against hope that she'd see through him and his insane defensive reactions.

At the same time, realizing this was his last chance. And he'd blown it, big time.

Sara's ears rang, deafening her as she smiled up at his face. "Rot in hell, Jack," she purred, sweetly, leaning up to kiss him and trace his lips with her tongue delighting in his taste, the richness of his lips while she let her anger take her somewhere else – anywhere but there. She spoke quietly against his ear, her hand caressing the back of his neck, twining into his hair. "You can take your creator ego bullshit and shove it. Trust me when I say you can fuck with the best of them too, but you will never be that – the best, that is – 'cause you can't see past your own dick to realize that no one will ever worship you like you worship yourself." He blinked at her words, and his face closed up again.

She knew she should stop, but had to prove to him that he could not toy with her.

"Because you know what? I think I've now had the best and he comes in a much blonder and better endowed package."

He reached for her, and she jumped away, her teeth clinched.

"Don't – ever – touch – me again."

She pushed past him to the door, threw it open, and heard the party from downstairs, as she took deep breaths to clear her head.

"Give my best to your boyfriend," he growled into her ear, as he walked by her. "Gotta go wrap up downstairs now, better run along and call him before he figures what you've been doing here with me for the last two hours," he turned back briefly to face her. "Stupid fucker should have never let you come here without him – I wouldn't have. Oh and tell him I said hey and that I can give him a few tips if he needs them,"

Tears blinded her and she slumped into the elevator, her last sight of Jack's eyes, bright with unshed tears before the doors slid shut.

EPILOGUE

Sara sat shivering and staring out the window of Blake's car. He'd picked her up at the airport from a two-week escape to her parents' condo in Florida. After sleepwalking through work for a week and avoiding Jack and Craig like the plague, she hopped on a plane on a whim and bolted, ashamed at herself but unable to handle the stress any other way, using Thanksgiving as an excuse for the trip. Another wave of nausea ripped through her, making her groan and lean her head against the cold glass. Blake patted her leg.

"Flu?" He turned into her condo's parking lot. She wiped her dry lips with the back of her hand and didn't say anything. Tossing her purse and laptop on the kitchen table, and noting how messy she'd left everything she made a mental note to get that back under control first thing.

Blake puttered around in her kitchen while she sat very still and tried like hell not to throw up. A chill passed through her and her head pounded, exacerbating the roiling in her gut that would not stop no matter what she ate or didn't eat.

"Eat this Sara. Damn, you must have lost fifteen pounds, what's your deal?" Her mind felt muddled, her body betrayed her in completely unfamiliar ways. She knew he was really worried about the dark circles under her eyes, her pale skin and inability to focus but just couldn't bring herself to tell him anything, too embarrassed by the whole fucking mess to admit anything.

"Sorry, just the tea, I can't keep anything down at all," she mumbled reaching for the steaming mug.

"Sara," she glanced up as Blake pulled the box clearly marked "early pregnancy test" from her bag. "What the hell is this?"

She stood and snatched it from him, starting for the bathroom. "Lose your ability to read words? What the hell does it look like? Thanks for the ride. You can go home now."

When she finally emerged, face numb from shock, mind spinning with terror, he still sat, mug in hand staring out the window as the snow piled up outside. He saw her and stood, pulling her into his arms.

"Shh, Sara, it's okay. It will all be fine."

Sara's body shook as he eased her to the couch, pressed her back and covered her with a blanket. Her eyes stayed dry and her mind cleared. She put a hand to her still flat stomach.

Mine. She thought, as a single tear slipped down her face. Blake wiped it away and smiled at her.

The End...

Closing Costs (Stewart Realty, Book 3)
Available from Sizzlin' Books

The minute he stepped into the back office hallway, Craig sensed something wasn't right. He dropped his helmet on a desk and started to the front, ignoring the strange emptiness of a normally busy summertime real estate office. A sharp, coppery odor stung his nose, making his heart race. As he sprinted around the corner separating the conference room from the open office area he heard it. Just a soft moan, then the slam of a door, then nothing. His ears started buzzing and his stride lengthened but the hall suddenly felt like ten miles of empty road.

As he approached the large conference room door he stopped. The only sounds were his own breathing and laughter from the storefront side of the office. But he sensed her there, somewhere.

"Sara?" His throat constricted when the knob wouldn't cooperate, but he wrestled it open. His first thought upon entering was that someone had spilled red paint all over the carpet. Once his brain fully registered the scene, he saw her, half under the table, curled in a ball and moaning. "Dear Christ, Sara." He sat down, grabbed her hand, pulled her into his lap, then watched in helpless horror as her eyes rolled back and felt her body spasm with a terrifying seizure. "Stay with me Sara. I mean it." He glanced up. Pam and Chris stood, phones in hand. "Somebody call a fucking ambulance already!"

As Sara's body calmed, he brushed her hair back, no longer caring he sat in a pool of her blood. His ears roared but he kept his voice soft. She opened her eyes, as tears dripped down her cheeks.

"Jack?"

He smiled, kissed her nose, the cloying odor of blood and fear clogging his brain. "No honey. It's Craig. Try to relax. I think there are some people here to take you to the hospital." The next few minutes passed like hours. Sara faded in and out of consciousness and the ogling crowd grew larger.

"Oh God it hurts...." Her loud moan ripped through his gut. When a hand touched his shoulder he jerked it away trying to focus on her.

"Sir, sir, please, let us handle this."

He started, then let the paramedic pull Sara off his lap. "Are you hurt?" The woman's eyes traveled up and down him as her partner laid Sara back and started taking her vital signs. He looked down at the apparent carnage reflected on his clothes. Her blood. So much of it. He swallowed hard.

"No, no, it's not me. I found her here like this, sat down and…." His brain focused. "Take her to U of M. I'll meet you there."

"Okay dad, calm down. We need to get her stabilized first." The woman patted his arm. By now the entire office had collected in the hallway, staring at the bloody scene. Craig struggled to comprehend what she said to him.

"Oh, no, I'm not," he looked up as Jack Gordon came barreling through the door separating the public from the private part of their sales office. "I mean, is she okay? She seized on me, about a minute."

"Yeah, her blood pressure is through the roof, pulse thready. She's lost way too much blood already. Let's get her out of here." The medics bustled around. "Excuse me sir, you need to move aside." Jack stood, staring at the room, mouth agape, eyes wild. Craig took in what the man saw: the floor darkened with Sara's blood and her back arched, feet kicking against the carpet as another seizure gripped her. He watched the man's face go utterly white, as he gripped the door knob. "Sir!" The medic shoved Jack out of the way and rolled the gurney in. Once she had stilled the two EMTs lifted her up and hustled her out into the waiting ambulance.

"You okay?" Craig narrowed his eyes at Jack.

"No." The other man turned, pushed his way through the gathered crowd and ran outside. Craig grabbed his helmet and rushed out behind Jack. Following the ambulance through midday streets, taking deep breaths to calm his heart, he forced himself to focus on the traffic while long forgotten prayers raced through his brain.

About Liz Crowe

Microbrewery owner, multi-published author, beer blogger and journalist, mom of three teenagers, and soccer fan, Liz brings years of real-world experience to her life as author. Working in sales and fund raising, plus an eight-year stint as an ex-pat trailing spouse PLUS making her way in a world of men (i.e. the beer industry) has given her all the "what if?" moments she needs for many books.

When she isn't sweating inventory and sales figures for the brewery, she can be found writing, editing or sweating promotional efforts for her latest publications. When free time presents itself you are likely to find her walking her standard poodles or doing Bikram yoga.

Her beer blog is nationally recognized for its insider yet outsider views on the craft beer industry. Her books are set in the not-so-common worlds of breweries, on the soccer pitch and in high powered real estate offices. Don't ask her for anything "like" a Budweiser or risk painful injury. If you want an education on all things beer related, follow her beer blog: **www.a2beerwench.com**

Liz Crowe's official website can be found at **www.lizcrowe.com** For all writing-related topics (including backlist titles, latest release updates, interviews, tour dates, and more) can be found at her **www.brewingpassion.com**.

Follow Liz:

Facebook: **www.facebook.com/lizcroweauthor**
Twitter: **@beerwencha2**

CPSIA information can be obtained at www.ICGtesting.com
Printed in the USA
LVOW132321010812

292588LV00007B/8/P